MASQUERADE MARRIAGE

Carlotta's headstrong waywardness had led her to make one bad mistake—a disastrous marriage to a man she barely knew, against her father's wishes. Now she had escaped from that and was safe on her tycoon father's yacht—but she didn't seem to be able to escape from Brad . . .

MASQUERADE MARRIAGE

BY

FLORA KIDD

MILLS & BOON LIMITED
15-16 BROOK'S MEWS
LONDON W1A 1DR

First published in Great Britain 1987 by Mills & Boon Limited

© Flora Kidd 1987

Australian copyright 1987 Philippine copyright 1987 This edition 1987

ISBN 0 263 75650 5

Set in Linotron Times 11 on 11 pt. 01-0487-49462

Typeset in Great Britain by Associated Publishing Services Printed and bound in Great Britain by Collins, Glasgow

CHAPTER ONE

ALONE and feeling lonely, Carlotta Burr, only daughter of Texas oil tycoon Mason J. Burr II and heiress to his millions, sat at one of the tables on the patio at Brock's marina on the Caribbean island of Morunda and watched the crowd of people who were dancing on the deck.

It was New Year's Eve and the dancers were celebrating the fact. They were a mixed lot, owners of yachts, captains and crews off charter yachts, charterers, regular tourists from the States, Canada, Europe and South America, local merchants and business people. The colours of their skins ranged from the tapeworm whiteness of those who had just arrived from the frozen north, the lobster pink of the newly sunburned, through amber, café-au-lait and mahogany to deep, enduring ebony black. Of many ethnic origins and nationalities, they were united that night in their determination to welcome the New Year with noise and movement.

They had abandoned the bar, restaurant and patio to dance on the wooden deck that jutted out over water. Even waitresses and waiters were dancing to the music of drums, guitars and electric organ. Some couples shuffled, clinging to each other. Others preferred to be separate as they stamped, twisted and rocked, their feet thumping on wood. And all the time Carlotta watched.

No one looking at Carlotta would have guessed she was disconsolate. Sitting straight, looking like a pale moth in her dress of white chiffon, her golden hair, thick and rippling with natural waves, held back from her high brow with a black velvet band and swirling about her shoulders, one foot in its black velvet pump tapping in time to the music, she appeared cool, elegant and possibly a little haughty. Her expensive clothes and her cared-for beauty set her apart from the other people at the party, and were probably the reasons why she had not been asked to dance.

Yet there was one other person not dancing. He sat at another table a few yards away from Carlotta's, his long legs stretched under the small table. He was leaning back in the chair and his hands were in the pockets of his white trousers so that his elbows had pushed back the white suit jacket he was wearing. Under the jacket he wore a round-necked blue T-shirt, part of the uniform that the members of the crew of the motor yacht *Montezuma*, owned by Mason J. Burr, always wore.

For a few moments Carlotta let her attention leave the dancers and concentrate on the man at the other table. High forehead across which a straight lock of sun-bleached dark brown hair fell, bold nose, square jaw, he wasn't bad looking, she thought—and had always thought when she had seen him moving about the yacht. It was strange how often she had seen him when she had been ashore, had caught glimpses of him on Front Street sauntering along on the other side of the street from herself, or in a shop where she had stopped to buy something, or even at the casino—the other night he had been at the roulette table. And now he was here, a few yards away from her, yet not looking at her and, like her, he wasn't dancing.

Voices coming from inside the dining-room drew her attention away from him. A group of people had arrived to join in the festivities offered by the marina management for the celebration of the New Year. They were well dressed, the women in evening gowns and jewels, the men in white tuxedos and bow-ties. They were all well dined and well wined too, judging by their laughter and noisy voices.

As they approached the archway that gave access from the dining-room to the patio Carlotta recognised them and stiffened. One of the women was Phillida Chalmers, also from Dallas, Texas, and a cousin of Carlotta's stepmother, Cora. With Phillida was Gordon Chalmers, a business colleague of Mason J. Burr. The other couple were the Digbys from New York, and with them was their son, Bernard, the one person Carlotta had hoped to avoid meeting that night by dining at the unpretentious marina restaurant instead of going with him to the New Year's Eve dinner and ball at the International Hotel, Morunda's most luxurious and exclusive rendezvous.

On sudden impulse, driven by her intense dislike of Bernard as well as a certain flicker of panic, Carlotta sprang to her feet and went over to the man who was lounging at the other table. She sat down on the chair next to his.

'The music has changed. They're playing a

slow waltz for the end of the old year,' she whispered, leaning close to him, her shoulder touching his. 'Please will you dance with me?'

He turned his head slowly. To her surprise his eyes were dark brown, widely spaced and long-lashed; for some reason she had expected him to have grey or light blue eyes. His thick, slightly peaked eyebrows lifted in surprise.

Behind her she heard Bernard's voice, too jovial, too loud, wine-slurred.

'Please,' she whispered. 'Please dance with me. I need your help.'

Surprise was followed by a frown. For one impatient moment she thought he was going to refuse. Then suddenly he smiled, his eyes glinted and his generously curved lips parted to show strong white teeth. Attractive dents appeared in his lean cheeks.

'OK. Let's dance,' he said softly.

They stood up together and walked to the edge of the patio. Bernard called to her.

'Hey, Carlotta,' he shouted above the sound of the music, and there was a clatter as he tipped over one of the wrought-iron chairs in his haste to detain her.

'Quick.' Carlotta took hold of her companion's hand and pulled him with her down the shallow steps to the deck. Turning to him, she lifted her arms and linked her fingers together behind his neck. 'Hold me close,' she murmured. 'Hold me as if you're used to dancing with me, as if we've known each other for a long time. I don't want to talk to him. I don't want to have anything to do with him. He's a brute, an animal, after one thing only, and I'm at my wits' end wondering how to fend him off, to get rid of him.'

To her great relief, her partner didn't argue. His hands curved to the shape of her waist, and his cheek, only slightly bristly with beard stubble, pressed against hers. His right leg pushed against her lcft leg and then they were off, moving in unison, drifting about the wooden boards among the other couples in time to the music of the Anniversary Waltz as played by the Caribbean combo.

'I suppose you know who I am,' Carlotta whispered. His ear was close to her lips and his skin smelt of scented soap. The heat of his hands at her waist in intimate contact penetrated through the thin stuff of her dress to her smooth skin.

'You're the daughter of Mason J. Burr II,' he replied. 'Owner of the yacht I'm crewing on. I guess you know I've been on the *Montezuma* for the past few weeks.'

'Of course I do. I wouldn't have asked you to dance with me if I hadn't known that. What's your name?'

'You can call me Brad.'

'I've seen you often, in places where I've been in the town. Have you been following me?' she asked.

'Why would I want to follow you?' he murmured. 'It's just been a coincidence that I've been in the same place that you have.'

'I suppose so.' They drifted some more among the other dancers. Then she said: 'Did you see the man who called out to me? Can you see him now?'

'Yes.'

'What's he doing?'

'He's standing at the top of the patio steps

and he's watching us.' He felt his shoulders
shake as he laughed. 'He looks like a bull is
supposed to look when it sees a red rag.'

'Bulls have poor eyesight,' she said seriously.
'It isn't the red colour that enrages them but any
sudden movement that they can't define clearly.
They charge at the movement because they're
afraid.'

'And you should know, I suppose, being the
daughter of a cattle rancher who also happens to
be the president of a Texas oil company,' he
remarked drily.

They turned slowly. Dancing in that way, in
entire body contact with him, was soothing,
thought Carlotta dreamily. She felt safe being
held by him, safer than she had felt for a long
time.

'Who's the bullish-looking guy, and why don't
you like him?' Brad asked, his breath wafting
some tendrils of her hair.

'He's Bernard Digby, and I've known him for
years. I don't like him because he's been taking
advantage of old acquaintance,' she replied,
somehow not finding it strange to confide in
him. 'He thinks that because we've known each
other for a long time he can make love to me
whenever he feels like it. The only way I've
been able to fend him off is to tell him my
husband will be here tonight. Now I'm sure he's
come to this dance to find out if Kurt has
arrived.' She pushed away from him a little so
she could look up at his face. Dappled by the
light that was shining out on to the deck though
the wide windows of the restaurant, his features
were ruggedly handsome. He looked tough

and self-assured, capable of dealing with any surprising or even dangerous event.

'I gather Kurt hasn't turned up,' he remarked, taking hold of her in a more conventional way, his right arm around her waist, his hand resting against her back while he took her right hand in his left as he whirled her in a traditional waltz movement.

'No, he hasn't. And he won't be coming,' she replied curtly, thinking how well Brad could dance, as if he had taken lessons in ballroom dancing at some time, guiding her through the movements easily, actually controlling where and how she moved. The experience was new for her. She had never met nor danced with a man who had taken over the direction of her dancing.

'Then you're in a bit of a fix, aren't you, princess?' he taunted. 'Caught out in a lie.'

'Why do you call me "princess"?' she demanded.

'Everyone around here calls you that.'

'Why?'

'Probably because you behave and look as they imagine a princess should.'

'But . . . that's silly. I'm just an ordinary person. I'm just like the other women of my own age who are here. I like to dance and have fun.'

'No, you're not like them. You're rich, an heiress to millions of dollars. That sets you apart from them.' He swung her around expertly, and the full skirt of her dress billowed out. 'Is it because your husband hasn't turned up that you need my help?' he asked.

'Yes. Please try to understand. I only lied to

Bernard in self-defence. It was all I could think of to disconcert him the other night.'

'What do you want me to do?'

'If Bernard comes over to us and starts being a nuisance would you mind pretending you are Kurt? It will only be for a few minutes.'

His eyebrows flickered in surprise and he pulled her close to him again. The whirling waltz steps stopped and they began the slow shuffle that all the other dancers were doing and which made it possible for them to talk without being overheard.

'I don't get this,' he said. 'Where is your husband? Have you left him? Or has he left you? Are you divorced or going to be? Or is he going to turn up eventually?'

'He isn't going to turn up, ever,' she said coldly and flatly. 'He died soon after we were married, in a hunting accident. Broke his neck. You don't need to know any more than that.'

'Oh, yes, I do,' he retorted. 'I need to know his last name if I am to pretend to be him even for a few minutes. I know you as Carlotta Burr. Didn't you change your last name when you married?'

'Yes, I did.' She was glad, she decided, that he hadn't bothered to commiserate with her over Kurt's death, to be hypocritical about it. 'But I decided to revert to Burr when I came out to Morunda.'

'Kurt sounds German,' he went on in a brisk businesslike manner, strange to find in a deckhand, she thought suspiciously. 'Was he a German?'

'He was Austrian. I met him at a horse show he was jumping in,' she said.   'I was jumping

in the same show. His last name was Malden.
You may have heard of him. He won a gold in
the last Olympic equestrian events.'

'No, I haven't heard of him. I don't follow the
horse-jumping shows or events closely,' he said
drily. 'So Malden is your married name. Doesn't
Bernard know that Kurt is dead?'

'You're very picky,' she complained. 'You
don't have to know everything. Just pretend to
be Kurt if Bernard comes over and tries to
accost me. Believe me he's quite capable of
cutting in and causing a scene if I refuse to
dance with him. Especially if he's smashed—and
I can tell he's been drinking.'

'Please excuse me for being "picky" as you
call it, princess,' he retaliated. 'But I like to be
prepared for any eventuality. You've just told
me Bernard is an old acquaintance of yours, so
why doesn't he know that Kurt is dead?'

'He doesn't know because the news of Kurt's
death hasn't been spread to my American friends.
Only my father knows, and he won't have told
anyone. Bernard was even surprised to find me
here when he arrived in Morunda last week.
Now, please will you do as I ask and pretend to
be Kurt if Bernard comes over?'

They made a few slow turns before he
answered. Carlotta couldn't help wishing that
they were dancing together because they wanted
to be dancing together, that this close-contact
waltzing was a dance of courtship which would
lead on to . . . Heavens, what was she doing,
letting her thoughts wander into the realms of
fantasy?

'How much?' her partner said softly and
succinctly in her ear.

'How much what?' Startled, she stiffened and pushed away from him again so she could see his face. His black-fringed dark eyes gazed down at her enigmatically.

'How much will you pay me for pretending to be your husband for a few minutes?' he asked smoothly.

'You'd want to be paid?' she gasped.

'I would. In US dollars, preferably. I never do anything for anyone for nothing,' he drawled. 'I'm a mercenary. My services are for hire only.'

A sense of deep disappointment washed through Carlotta, to be followed quickly by a feeling of cold cynicism. She should have known, she thought. Whenever other people met her they saw dollar signs immediately, and wondered how much they could take her for.

'You've already been hired by Skipper Atkins and through him by my father to serve as a crew on the yacht,' she reminded him icily. 'I don't see why I should pay you anything.'

'But when I was hired no mention was made of me having to pretend to be your husband for a few minutes,' he argued mockingly. 'Now, I value my state of single blessedness very highly. Pretending to be married to you would mean I'd have to give up that single state, so if you want me to do it you'll have to pay.'

Dismayed by his tough bargaining, Carlotta was silent as he whirled her around again. What should she do now? Go on with the idea? Tell him she was willing to hire him for the next half-hour for so many dollars? Or should she step back, ask him to forget she had ever approached him, stop dancing with him and turn to face Bernard's leers?

Before she could decide, the music stopped suddenly with a loud chord from the electric organ. It was midnight. The old year had gone and the New Year was in. Everyone was suddenly wishing everyone else a happy New Year and kissing. The hooters of cargo ships in the harbour were sounding and fireworks were shooting up into the sky to fall in coloured and blazing white showers of sparks above the black outlines of the hills. The band began to play *Auld Lang Syne* and everyone began to make circles holding hands. A heavy hand slapped down on Carlotta's bare shoulder and she gasped. Bernard's voice boomed.

'Happy New Year, Carlo,' he yelled. 'How about a kiss?'

He began to push between her and her partner. She could see his thick lips gleaming lasciviously and his protruding pale eyes leering at her. She began to back away from him but quite suddenly he was shoved back by her partner, who stepped up to her, swept her against him and kissed her hard on the lips.

'Happy New Year,' he whispered, his dark eyes dancing with wicked mockery when he raised his head.

'Who the hell is this guy?' Bernard demanded pompously.

'I'm Kurt Malden. Who are you?' said Carlotta's partner, much to her relief.

'I told you Kurt would turn up today, Bernie,' she said smiling brightly to hide the sudden laughter that was bubbling up inside her at the expression of amazement on Bernard's round, fleshy face. She thought he looked like a small boy who had just had his favourite toy taken

away from him by another child. 'Are you having
a good time?' she went on. 'We are. It's been
great fun here . . .'

'So this is where you've been hiding this
evening, Carlotta,' said another voice, a high-
pitched woman's voice that Carlotta recognised
only too well. Her heart beating twenty to the
dozen, her cheeks flaming suddenly red, she
turned to face Phillida Chalmers reluctantly. Tall
and stately in a long blue gown, white curls
glittering like frozen foam, blue eyes narrow
between mascaraed eyelashes, Phillida was looking not at Carlotta but at the man standing close
to her, his arm around her waist. 'We were
expecting you to join us at the International for
dinner,' Phillida went on rather reprovingly.
'You were invited, you know, but when you
didn't turn up Bernie suggested we would find
you here.'

For only a moment Carlotta panicked, and
nearly gave in to the desire to run away from
them all rather than continue with the masquerade
which she had initiated only to protect her from
Bernard. It would be crazy to go on with it.
Then she caught sight of Bernard's face: he was
leering at her sceptically as if he had guessed the
truth about her dancing partner. That expression
was all she needed to make her go on recklessly
with the pretence without a thought as to any
consequences that might arise.

'Hello, Phillida,' she replied lightly. 'I'd have
come to dinner with you, only Kurt arrived.'
She turned to Brad and gazed up at him, hoping
that the expression on her face was appropriately
adoring. 'Darling,' she murmured, feeling wild
laughter spurting up inside her at her own daring

in using the endearment to this stranger. 'I'd like you to meet Phillida Chalmers. Phillida, this is Kurt, my husband. He flew in from Europe this afternoon. When did you arrive on the island?'

'We flew from Miami this afternoon.' Phillida held out her right hand to Brad. 'So pleased to meet you, Kurt, at last. We have all heard of Carlotta's runaway marriage to you and wondered if we would ever be allowed to meet you.'

'I'm pleased to meet you, Mrs Chalmers,' said the counterfeit Kurt—and Carlotta was surprised to hear him speak with what could have passed as an Austrian accent.

Suddenly, behind her and Brad the circling dancers broke up into couples and singles again. There was a lot of cheering and people rushed towards the patio steps as they made for the bar where free champagne was being served to welcome the New Year.

'Well, really, what a lot of ruffians,' complained Phillida, grasping Bernard's arm to regain her balance when she was almost knocked down by one of the dancers. 'I can't think why you want to be here, Carlotta. We came over in two cars, so why don't you and Kurt drive with us to the villa, right now? It's so lovely up there on a moonlit night. We can talk without interruption and you can both stay the night. You know we have plenty of room . . .'

'Thank you for the kind invitation,' Brad spoke with cool authority, 'but Carlotta and I would prefer to go back to the yacht. We haven't been together for some weeks and we have some catching up to do, haven't we, *sweetheart*?'

His arm tightened around her waist and his

dark eyes slanted a sultry glance down at her
upturned face. Again she felt the desire to laugh.
She was enjoying deceiving Phillida and Bernard,
both of whom she disliked so much, and
there was a certain excitement in sharing the
masquerade with someone as quick-witted and
self-confident as Brad seemed to be.

'Yes, we have, darling,' she murmured and
leaned her head against his shoulder as she
smiled at Phillida. 'Please excuse us, both of
you. We'd like to dance some more and then go
to bed.'

'We could stay,' Bernard suggested quickly.
'It's more fun here, Phillida . . .'

'You can stay if you want, Bernie.' Phillida
had to shout because the band had started up
again, playing a boisterous Caribbean number
with a strong rocking rhythm. 'I can't stand this
noise and I'm sure Gordon and your parents
can't either. We're leaving. Good night, Carlotta,
Kurt. I'll come over to see you tomorrow.'

Turning on her heel Phillida marched towards
the patio and was almost knocked down again as
dancers rushed back to the deck to stamp and
rock to the lively beat of the music. And
suddenly Carlotta found herself whirling round
and round securely held by her partner in the
deception she had just enacted.

She was whirled away from the bewildered yet
suspicious Bernard, guided expertly among the
other dancers until they were all between her
and Bernard. Right to the end of the deck she
was whirled, to the place where the first concrete
dock of the marina joined it, and the shadows of
the marina buildings were thick and black.

They stopped dancing and stood still, both of them breathing hard, facing each other.

'Thanks,' said Carlotta when she had breath enough for speech. 'Thank you for helping out. Bernard's face was a picture when you said you were Kurt. He was absolutely stunned. I wanted to laugh so much.'

He let go of her and pushed his hands in his trouser pockets. There wasn't much light where they were standing, although beyond the shadows everything was silvered by the radiance of the full moon now sailing high in the clear midnight blue of the tropical sky. She could see that he was frowning at her.

'How . . . how much do you want me to pay you?' she asked, remembering his demand just before Bernard had wished her a happy New Year.

'That depends on how long you want the pretence to continue,' he replied curtly.

'What do you mean?' She spoke sharply. 'I told you it would be for a few minutes, for Bernard's benefit.'

'Then it was hardly wise of you to introduce me as your husband to Phillida Chalmers, was it? Especially since she's going to call to see you tomorrow.' His voice rasped drily. 'You're in it now, right up to your neck, *sweetheart*.' Sarcasm edged his voice as he spoke the endearment. 'It won't take long for her to find out I'm not your husband but only a deckhand on your father's yacht. And I wouldn't be surprised if your pursuer, Bernard, doesn't start checking on me tonight. All he has to do is go to the yacht and ask if Kurt Malden is on board. Hadn't you thought of that?'

'No, I hadn't,' she admitted frankly. She hadn't thought beyond the impulse that had led her to ask him to play the part of Kurt. Invaded by panic and a sort of moon-madness, she hadn't thought at all. 'I didn't think . . .'

'I bet you never do,' he interrupted unkindly. 'I bet you're always rushing into situations without thinking. I'd take a guess too that your runaway marriage to Kurt was one of them. It didn't work out the way you wanted so you rushed out of it, rushed back to Daddy, to his yacht where you could hide. Or thought you could hide, but unfortunately Bernard turned up and started to pester you!'

'Shut up,' she hissed furiously. 'You've no right to speak to me like that. No right to criticise me.'

'Excuse me.' His voice drawled mockingly. 'I forgot my position. I forgot I'm only one of your father's employees and likely to lose my job if he finds out from Skip Atkins that I've been impersonating your husband.'

'Oh, no!' Carlotta exclaimed. 'I don't want that to happen. I don't want Phillida or Bernard to find out I've deceived them. At least, not yet. And I don't want you to lose your job.' She broke off as she heard footsteps coming towards them. A high-shouldered, big-headed figure in a white tuxedo was coming towards them. 'Bernard. He's coming this way!' she whispered. 'What shall we do?'

For answer Brad seized her hand in a rough sinewy grasp and made for the steps that led down from the deck to the beach, pulling her after him.

CHAPTER TWO

BEFORE them the beach of yellow sand that curved around the head of the wide bay was lit by the moon. It was possible to walk along the sand to the town of Morrisburg, Morunda's capital and port, instead of going by road. Now, the lights from the houses and hotels in the town glittered like jewels against the dark slopes of the hills behind it, and fireworks sent up in celebration of the New Year blossomed in the sky, red, white and blue.

There were no shadows on the beach where Carlotta and Brad walked hand in hand. Anyone standing on the marina deck would see them.

'I should have guessed he wouldn't go to the villa with the others. I should have guessed he would stay around to spy on me,' Carlotta murmured bitterly. She glanced over her shoulder quickly. 'Oh, he's following us, coming down the steps.'

'He doesn't seem to be as stunned or as convinced as you'd hoped he would be,' said Brad calmly, not looking back at all, seeming completely unconcerned.

'I don't want him to start bothering us now,' complained Carlotta. 'Oh, let's hurry away from him.'

'No.' His grasp on her hand tightened. 'If we

start showing panic by running away from him he'll guess he's on to something.' He swung her round to face him. 'Best to do something to put him off the scent. Such as this.'

Dropping her hand, he framed her face with both his hands and before she could do or say anything to stop him he kissed her. Her first instinct was to resist, to push him away, but his hands left her face and caught her wrists roughly. He twisted her arms behind her back forcing her body against his. While dancing with him she hadn't objected to the close contact, but now the roughness of his actions awoke an oft-smothered memory within her. She shuddered and stiffened.

At once he lifted his lips from hers and whispered softly and sardonically. 'You're not the most loving wife in the world, sweetheart. How about relaxing a little and showing Bernard just how glad you are that I've turned up tonight and that I'm here to protect you from his over-amorous attentions?'

One of his hands left her wrists and slid up her back slowly, the heat of it seeming to burn through the thin chiffon. His fingers wound in her hair, grasping a bunch of the silky strands so tightly that it would have hurt her to turn her face away from his.

'Now, when I kiss you again, kiss me back,' he whispered. 'I'm sure you really know how.'

His lips touched hers and she shuddered again, not because she disliked the feel of his lips so much but because ever since Kurt's horrible and frightening mauling of her on their wedding night she had hated being touched by a man.

Being kissed caused a cold, hard knot of loathing to form inside her.

'Kiss me,' Brad ordered again against her lips and held her closer to him. Closing her eyes tightly, she pressed her lips to his, then slowly raised her arms and put them round his neck. The hair at the back of his neck felt thick and silky.

It would be over soon, she told herself. It wasn't going to last for long, just long enough to convince Bernard that Brad was really her husband Kurt, and she was unprepared for the way Brad's lips began to move experimentally over hers, exploring their softness and then parting them so that his tongue could flicker briefly yet tantalisingly against the tip of hers.

The teasing touch of his tongue seemed to send a scalding heat through her that melted the knot and danced flamelike through the lower part of her body. As he had suggested she relaxed against him and immediately her body was invaded by a host of new sensations. She felt the strong beat of his heart striking through to her breast, the pressure of his long fingers in one of her buttocks, the thrust of one of his knees between hers. From being a masquerade kiss, a pretence merely to convince Bernard, the embrace was fast developing into a sensuous experience that she was enjoying. Seduced by the warmth of his lips and the touch of his hands, she clung to him, licking his lips, savouring the taste of them, inhaling the scents of his skin and hair until she felt a little giddy.

As if he also sensed the kiss was going on too long and was possibly getting out of control, Brad lifted his head abruptly.

'OK, that will do,' he whispered scoffingly. 'No need to overact. Bernard's gone.'

His withdrawal and cool, mocking remarks had a devastating effect on her. She felt as if she had been rejected. Bewildered by the feeling, her hands at her hot cheeks, she stepped back from him quickly and glanced round. It was true Bernard was no longer up there watching. Nor was he walking towards them over the soft sand. Bewilderment faded, its place being taken by anger.

Turning to face Brad she raged in a whisper, 'Don't ever do that again. It wasn't necessary to kiss me.' She wiped the back of her hand across her bruised and trembling lips. 'I don't like being kissed.'

'So it seems,' he retorted.

He was casual again, an unconcerned stranger, hands in his trouser pockets and head bent so that the long, recalcitrant lock of straight hair slid forward on to his forehead. With one foot he was pushing around a piece of dry, washed-up seaweed. He was even whistling softly between his teeth, the tune the band was playing now, a song by Stevie Wonder, which was a favourite of hers.

'*I just called to say I love you.*' The voices of the dancers singing the popular lyric floated down and Carlotta winced. Once she had believed Kurt loved her. She had believed also that she had loved him. Now she knew that there had been no real love between them, but only infatuation on her part and greed on his, both of which had changed to hate and frustration under pressure.

She glanced at Brad again. He had stopped

whistling and was no longer playing with the seaweed. Straight and still, he was watching her, his dark eyes pools of blackness in his moon-silvered face. She had the impression that he was watching her with concern and interest. But, then, he was probably only waiting to be paid, she thought wryly.

I'll see you tomorrow,' she said coolly. 'I'll pay you then. In American dollars, of course.'

She turned and walked back to the deck. Going up the steps she held her head high, her slim shoulders straight. The tempo of the music tempted her momentarily to join the dancers again, but the thought that Bernard might be among them, dancing either with one of the girls off the charter yachts or sitting on the patio, watching and drinking, deterred her.

Reaching the concrete dock where the *Montezuma* was tied up, she paused watching the dancers enviously, wishing she were one of them, wishing above all that she wasn't who she was. Wild impulses flitted through her mind. Ignoring them with difficulty, she turned and began to walk along the dock past the bows and sterns of the yachts tied up in the berths. Some boats were dark and deserted. Others had light streaming out from cabin windows and people sitting around in cockpits and on decks, talking, laughing, still welcoming the New Year. Several voices called out to her as she passed. Someone even invited her aboard to have a drink. Shaking her head in refusal, she walked on.

Behind her a pleasantly deep voice with an English accent said, 'Very sensible of you, if I may say so, to refuse any invitations at this hour and to return to the yacht.'

Brad caught up with her, loped along beside her.

'I don't really care what your opinion is of my behaviour,' she said haughtily. It was time to put him back in his place as a deckhand employed by her father. 'Please don't speak to me or walk with me. And you don't have to come back to the yacht with me.'

'I want to make sure you don't go out again tonight,' he replied. 'And that you won't involve me in any more pretences.'

She didn't answer him. It was becoming very clear to her that he was one of those odious people she couldn't possibly get the better of in a verbal exchange. She walked on towards the *Montezuma*. Seventy-five feet of gleaming white paint, stainless steel fittings and glass windows, a great white whale of a power cruiser, it tugged gently at the ropes that tied it to the dock.

The gate in the port rail was open. As Carlotta stepped through it on to the main deck, a man came out of the doorway of the main saloon. He was stockily built and dressed in white shorts and a white shirt.

'Good night, Skip,' Carlotta said, and made her way to the stairs that led to the lower deck, the after cabins and stateroom.

'Good night, miss.' Skipper Atkins, who had been captain of the yacht for the four years Mason J. Burr had owned it, was, as always, briskly polite. Before she reached the stairs she heard him say to the man who had been with her, 'I'd like a word with you, Brad. Something queer has happened.'

'All right. Be with you in a few minutes,' answered the deckhand, who didn't sound at all subservient. 'Just as soon as I've seen Miss Burr to her cabin.'

She swung to face him as he came after her.

'You don't have to see me anywhere,' she whispered angrily. 'I can look after myself. I'm grown up!'

'You could have fooled me—about being grown up, I mean,' he taunted and smiled at her, disconcerting her. There was something about the way he smiled at her that destroyed the desire to rebel against him. Instead, she discovered she wanted to please him by doing exactly what he suggested.

With a little exclamation of irritation she turned and ran down the stairs and along the narrow carpeted passage to her cabin. Opening the door, she stepped over the sill and into the room, slamming the door shut after her and leaning against it.

After a while, when nothing happened, she moved across to the porthole. It was slightly open and she could still hear the music from the deck. Her foot tapped in time to the beat and rebelliousness stirred within her again, an old, familiar restlessness. Now she was wishing she hadn't returned to the yacht but had joined the dancers. Or, better than going to the marina and perhaps running into Bernard, she wished she had gone along the beach to Morrisburg to dance there in one of the discothèques. If she hadn't been so bewildered by Brad's behaviour she might have persuaded him to go with her. They could have danced together all night until their feet and legs had ached if he hadn't kissed her.

She could still go into the town. She didn't need him around to escort her. Hardly had the

impulse flared up than she had spun around and
was on her way to the door. Her hand closed
around the brass knob. She pushed. The door
remained shut. She pushed again, her shoulder
against the panels. It didn't open. Yet it wasn't—
it couldn't possibly be locked! But if it wasn't
locked, why didn't it open?

Raising her clenched fists, she banged on the
door and shouted to be let out. Her horror of
being locked in or restrained in any way surged
through her and had to be expressed in violent
action. But for all the noise she made no one
came, and she realised that no one would hear
her. Skipper Atkins was in the saloon with Brad,
and perhaps Jilly, the first mate, was there too.
Willy, the other deckhand, was probably ashore
still celebrating the New Year.

But there was still the bathroom door. Of
course! Why hadn't she thought of that instead
of wasting breath and energy banging on this
door! *I bet you never think*. Brad's jeer rang
through her mind. Perhaps he was right. She
didn't think. She'd never had to.

She flitted over to the doorway that led into
the small bathroom attached to her cabin. Across
the tiny room she went to the outer door, turned
its knob and pushed. The door remained closed,
Golden-brown, like the door of her cabin, shiny
with varnish, it was solid and it didn't open. It
too was locked.

But who would lock both doors from the
outside? Had Brad locked them? Had he followed
her after all, even though she had ordered him
not to see her to her cabin, and had he locked
her in?

How? How could he, who was only a

deckhand, have the keys to lock the doors? Only if Skip Atkins had given him the keys. Only if the keys had been taken from inside the doors at some time. That is if there had been any keys in the locks. She didn't really know if there had because she had never looked. She had never thought to lock her doors at night or at any other time.

Returning to the cabin, she flung herself down on the wide bunk and kicked off her velvet pumps. The music from the marina drummed through her head, and in an agony of frustration she beat at the pillow under the bunk cover with her fists.

Why had she been locked in? Why? Who had locked her in? If Brad had locked her doors, on whose orders had be been acting? What was it Skip Atkins had said to him? That something queer had happened? Something to do with her? Had the skipper ordered the deckhand to lock her in her rooms for the night? Who would give the skipper orders to lock her in if something occurred that made it necessary, for her own safety? Only the owner of the yacht, of course, her father.

Carlotta sighed irritably and shifted into a more comfortable position, her head on the pillow. She knew her father was concerned about her welfare. He always had been. It had been his idea that she should come to Morunda and stay on the *Montezuma* instead of going to Texas. She had phoned him from England, from the home of his cousin Grace Heward where she had gone after she had left Kurt.

'I'll advise Atkins that you're coming,' Mason J. Burr had said, delighted that she had left

Kurt. 'Stay on the yacht as long as you like. Stay there until I can get away and fly down to see you. And don't tell anyone you're going there!'

'I'll have to tell Grace,' she had interrupted him. 'She'll want to know where I'm going.'

'That's OK. Grace won't tell anyone. She's as close as they come, respects privacy. I want it kept out of the gossip columns, sugar. I don't want anyone to know where you are and above all I don't want that creep Kurt following you.'

It was then she had told him about Kurt's unexpected death in a fall when he had been training a new horse. The news of the accident had filtered through to her along the grapevine of the show-jumping community. Since no one had known she had married Kurt Malden secretly, information of his death had not been communicated to her directly, and apparently he hadn't told anyone back in Vienna that he had married the Burr heiress.

Although she had left Kurt the day after they had married and had been determined to divorce him somehow as soon as she could, the news that he had died with such abrupt violence had shocked Carlotta severely and she was sure that if she hadn't had the support of Grace she would have been ill. Coming as it had so soon after that other shock, the shock of her wedding night, the news could have caused her to have a nervous breakdown, if Grace, calm, shrewd Grace, hadn't pointed out to her that Kurt's death could have happened anyway, even if he hadn't been married to her, that she should put all past mistakes behind her and look forward to the future.

Restlessly she flung over on to her back. It was to avoid moments like these when she relived the recent past that she had helped Grace at the stables in Berkshire while she had stayed there. Every day she had mucked out stables, groomed horses or gone riding as far as she had been able, trying to tire herself so that she would fall asleep as soon as her head hit the pillow.

Here too, staying on the yacht, she had indulged in physical activities every day, swimming and snorkelling, playing tennis, windsurfing, and dancing at the various hotels and discos, doing anything to stop herself from remembering the mistake she had made in marrying Kurt.

She had first met him four years ago when she had been eighteen and jumping at a horse show in the States. It had been her first venture into international show-jumping events. After that first one, flushed with success, encouraged by her father and grandmother, backed by plenty of money and owning fine horses, she had gone on to compete in many events in the States and Europe. At all of them she met Kurt.

He had been ten years older than her, coolly sophisticated, with smooth, jet-black hair and black eyes. He had told her that he was descended from a long line of Austrian aristocrats and he had won more awards for show jumping than she could remember.

When he had shown an interest in her she had been flattered. Hero-worship had developed rapidly into infatuation for him, and so when he had proposed marriage to her last September she had been so delighted that she had accepted his proposal immediately.

They had been in Vienna at the time, both attending some horse trials there. She had phoned her father and told him her news. Mason J. Burr had flown out to Vienna to meet Kurt, had taken an instant dislike to the accomplished equestrian and had forbidden Carlotta to marry him.

'You can't forbid me to marry,' she had stormed at him. 'I'm twenty-one, nearly twenty-two. I can marry Kurt if I want and you can't stop me.'

'All I'm asking you to do, honey, is to slow down a little. To think about it. Marriage is a serious step and you don't know this guy too well.'

'I've known him for nearly four years.'

'But only off and on. You've only met him at these horse affairs. You know nothing about his background . . .'

'Yes, I do. I do! I know he comes from a very good family.'

'Have you met any of them?'

'No. All his nearest relatives are dead. He . . . he's alone in the world. And I don't need to know about his background. I love him and I'm going to marry him no matter what you say about him. You're always the same. You always dislike any guy who takes an interest in me.'

'Bide your time, then,' he had argued, quite reasonably she realised now, looking back. 'Get engaged but don't get married in a hurry. Get to know him better. You might change your mind.'

'No. I won't. I'll never change my mind, and

I'm going to marry him as soon as I can and you can't do anything about it.'

Mason J. Burr hadn't stayed to argue. He had left Vienna abruptly and she had lied to Kurt, had told him that her father had agreed to their marriage. Within a week they had flown to Paris and had been married there in a secret civil ceremony. Before the ceremony she'd cabled her father to inform him of the wedding, inviting him to attend. He hadn't flown to Paris but had sent a cable in return. It had been waiting for her when she and Kurt had arrived at the honeymoon suite, in a luxury Paris hotel, that she had booked.

'If you marry Malden you allowance will automatically stop and I shall cut you out of my will.'

The stark message of her father's cable seemed to be branded on her mind. She had shown the cable to Kurt. It had been a foolish thing to do, she could see that now. It would have been better to have waited a while, until the marriage had been consummated, until they had settled into a relationship.

She would never forget the effect of the cable on Kurt. Never. The elegant aristocrat had disintegrated before her eyes. He had become a foul-mouthed bully who had accused her of leading him to believe she was wealthy and would always be wealthy, of trapping him into a marriage he didn't want now that he knew she would be disinherited.

'But . . . I thought . . . we married today because we . . . we love each other,' she had stammered and going to him had put her arms around him. 'Money isn't all that important . . .'

'No. Not to someone like you who has always had more than enough,' he had snarled at her. 'As for love.' He had laughed jeeringly at her. 'There's no such thing.'

'I love you. I wouldn't have married you if I didn't,' she had argued.

'Rubbish, romantic rubbish,' he had jibed. 'A cover-up women like you use to disguise sexual desire. You've deceived me, trapped me with your wealth, so you're going to find out now just what you've let yourself in for . . .'

What had happened next she had been trying to forget ever since. Oh, their marriage had been consummated all right, in the worst possible way, in a spirit of revenge. Kurt had taken her without tenderness or respect, without love, and next morning early, before he had been awake she had packed her bags, paid the bill and left Paris to fly to London. She had gone straight to the home of Grace Heward.

Three months had gone by since that awful night in Paris and she still felt frozen inside, still stiffened and retreated when a man showed an interest in her, when someone like Bernard came on to her . . .

She turned again on to her side and closed her eyes. The music from the marina deck beat through her brain and suddenly she was dancing again with Brad, feeling safe in his arms as he whirled her around. She was spinning down and down into darkness, around and around. She fell asleep.

CHAPTER THREE

HAVING been lulled to sleep by the distant throb of drums and guitars, Carlotta was awakened by the closer, more workmanlike throb of the *Montezuma's* powerful Rolls-Royce engines. Without opening her eyes, she stretched lazily and wondered vaguely why they had been started up. Then she turned over, snuggled her head into the pillow and tried to go to sleep again.

There was a knock on the door of the cabin. She opened her eyes, aware of a vague memory of the door having been locked from the outside when she had tried to open it last night. Knuckles rapped on the door again. She sat up and realised she had slept on top of the bunk cover and that she was still wearing the white chiffon dress. This morning it looked like a rag.

She swung her legs off the bed and went towards the door intending to shout through the thick wood that she couldn't open the door because it was locked from the outside. She had almost reached it when the brass knob turned slowly and the door was pulled open. In the passageway outside, Jilly Atkins, the skipper's wife who was also first mate and cook, stood, her round, cheerful face puckered in a slight frown of puzzlement. She was dressed in the crisp, white shorts and navy blue T-shirt that all the *Montezuma's* crew wore as their uniform, and on the palm of one hand she was carrying a small, round tray on which there stood a large glass of orange juice, the drink that Carlotta preferred when she woke up.

'Good morning, miss,' Jilly said, a bright smile replacing the frown, 'and a happy New Year.'

'Thanks, Jilly. And a happy New Year to you.' Carlotta took the tray and put it on a shelf beside the bunk. She was aware that Jilly was now looking in surprise at the creased and rag-like chiffon dress. 'I was so tired after dancing last night,' she was quick to explain, 'that I lay down and fell asleep before I had time to undress. I've only just woken up. What time is it?'

'Nine o'clock, give a minute or two either way,' replied Jilly. Her brown hair was cut very short, shingled at the back and spraying out in all directions on top of her head. Small gold buttons decorated the lobes of her ears. Not very tall, she was broad-shouldered and athletic-looking, and Carlotta knew after spending only a few weeks on board that Jilly was a competent and fearless navigator and sailor, as well as an excellent gourmet cook.

'Why are the engines going?' Carlotta asked, after sipping some of the juice. Freshly squeezed from Florida oranges, as she liked it, the juice pricked her palate, washing away the dryness that had developed in her mouth during sleep.

'The skipper has decided to take the ship for a spin through the islands. He'll tell you all about it when you come up for breakfast,' replied Jilly. 'He said it's time to blow the cobwebs out of them, that they've been idle long enough.'

'Good idea,' murmured Carlotta, then added quickly as Jilly moved towards the door, 'wait a minute, please. How did you open the door just now? Do you have a key to unlock it?'

Jilly's eyes opened wide in surprise. She looked down at the brass knob and the brass-edged keyhole below it.

'It wasn't locked, miss. The key is usually on the inside of the door.' She looked back at Carlotta, her eyes puzzled. 'Did you lock the door, miss? After you came in?'

'No. And to tell the truth I've never noticed a key in the lock on the inside of the door. I've never even thought of locking the door. But last night when I came back from the restaurant I decided to go out again. I couldn't because the door was locked. From the outside. I banged and shouted but no one heard me. It was the same with the door from the bathroom.'

'Well, I never,' exclaimed Jilly, whose real name was Jillian. Like her husband, she was English, and had once told Carlotta that she was born and grew up in the city of Liverpool. Although she hadn't lived in England for several years she still had a Liverpool accent, and her speech was sprinkled with English idioms. Before applying for the jobs of captain and first mate on the *Montezuma*, she and Stan had both worked on a British cruise ship, he as first mate and she as chief stewardess.

'Sometimes I've noticed that the doors on the yacht stick,' she continued now, pleasantly, as if wishing to reassure Carlotta. 'They swell in the heat and humidity. If you'd given the door a good shove . . .'

'I did.' Carlotta cut in impatiently. 'It wasn't

sticking. Neither of them were. They were locked.'

'Then you'd better tell Stan about it,' said Jilly. 'He might have locked them.' She grinned. 'I wouldn't put it past him,' she added mysteriously. 'Excuse me, now, miss. I must go and cook the breakfast.'

Jilly left the cabin and Carlotta finished drinking her orange juice and put the glass back on the tray.

Dragging the black velvet band from her head, she shook out her hair. Like a cloak of golden silk it swirled about her face and shoulders. Noticing the black velvet pumps she had kicked off the night before, she picked one of them up and examined it curiously. Grains of sand clung to the soft velvet. So she hadn't imagined all that had happened. She had walked down to the beach from the marina deck and she had been kissed, very thoroughly and quite unnecessarily kissed by a stranger.

Dropping the shoe, she stripped off the white dress and her underclothing and ran nude into the bathroom. A few minutes later, after a quick hot shower, she returned to the main cabin, her wet hair clinging to her body. She dressed quickly again in white shorts and a scarlet shirt, wound her still wet hair up into a knot on top of her head, found her sunglasses, slipped on sandals, and with a scarlet leather handbag slung over one shoulder she left the cabin and went up to the main deck and the saloon.

Through the wide windows of the saloon she could see the buildings of the marina hotel appearing, white walls and red roof shining in the bright sunlight, glowing against the green scrub of cacti and small bushes that covered the high hillside behind them. The expanse of water between the yacht and the land was a brilliant jade green glittering with yellow sunbeams.

In one corner of the big saloon there was a dining area. A cushioned settee berth covered in biscuit-coloured tweed curved about an oval table that was already set with two place mats, cutlery and blue plates. Skipper Atkins entered the saloon and came over to the table. He was carrying his peaked cap under one arm and, watching him from her corner of the settee, Carlotta thought, as always, that he and Jilly must have come out of the same mould. They were the masculine and feminine versions of the same character, both short and energetic, both pale-eyed and brown-haired, both speaking with the same accent.

'Good morning, miss.' Stan Atkins sat opposite her, on one of the upholstered chairs which were attached to the floor. Since she had arrived on the yacht he had breakfasted with her every morning. It seemed to be some sort of custom for the captain of the yacht to take the first meal of the day with the owner or representative of the owner, and she wondered who had started the custom on the *Montezuma*—her father, or this sharp-eyed Englishman?

'It's a lovely day,' he said cheerfully after she had acknowledged his greeting. 'I hope you didn't have anything planned to do ashore this morning. I suppose I should have asked you before we cast off from the dock.'

'Yes, you should have,' retorted Carlotta, but she smiled at him as she spoke. 'But I'm quite happy to get away from the marina this morning. Are you aiming for anywhere in particular?'

'Not really. I thought I'd leave that to you, miss. Where would you like to go?'

'St Phipps,' said Carlotta without hesitation. St Phipps was a sister island to Morunda, and both came under the same government. 'The Bay of Doves. Have you ever heard of Stewart Stenson?'

'Wasn't he that crazy recluse who inherited millions from his grandfather and then went about spending all the money on nutty projects? A bit like Howard Hughes?'

'That's right. He bought a whole headland in the Bay of Doves, built a house there and landscaped the area with all kinds of tropical trees and shrubs,' said Carlotta. 'It's now called Stenson Point after him, and the father of a friend of mine from Dallas has bought the estate. I'd like to see it. Is the anchorage in the Bay of Doves any good? I mean, is there enough depth of water for the *Monte*?' She used her father's shortened and affectionate version of the yacht's name.

'There's enough,' said the skipper. 'The entrance is a bit tricky, strewn with rocks, but once you're in you can anchor close to the shore. There's good snorkelling too, off the Point of Doves, opposite Stenson Point.'

'So can we go there now and stay the night there?' Carlotta was eager. It was just possible her friend Tizzy Carter, whose father had bought the Stenson estate, might be there, and it would be good to see Tizzy again. Nearly two years had passed since she had last seen her friend: two years during which she had gone with Kurt from one equestrian competition to the next, with never a thought for old friends.

'Of course we can. We can go wherever you want. You're the boss when your dad isn't on board,' replied the skipper with a twinkle.

'Am I?' Carlotta spoke drily. 'I wonder. I got the impression last night that my father's wishes and orders where I'm concerned stretch right down here from Texas.'

'Miss Burr couldn't open the doors of her cabin last night,' Jilly said, having overheard Carlotta's remarks as she brought two silver serving dishes to the table and set them down. 'She couldn't get out.'

'Oh? When was this?' queried the skipper, lifting off one of the covers. 'Mmm. Bacon and kidneys. Help yourself, miss.'

'After I'd returned to the yacht. Just after I'd seen you,' replied Carlotta, serving herself. 'I decided to go out again but couldn't get out. Both doors were locked from the outside.'

'They were probably sticking,' said the skipper blandly, heaping food on to his plate. 'I'll have Willy look at them.'

'They weren't sticking. They were locked,' Carlotta insisted, frowning at him fiercely, her slanting dark eyebrows taking on even more of a slant, her lower lip thrusting out.

The skipper didn't bat an eyelid. Round and clear his eyes looked straight back at her.

'The keys to the cabin doors are always on the inside for the use of the occupants of the cabins, so that they can lock their doors at night after they have retired to bed or, if they wish, to lock from the outside when they go ashore and take the keys with them,' he said coolly. 'Now, are you sure you didn't lock the doors yourself when you returned to the cabin and forget they were locked when you tried to go out?'

'Oh, come on, Skip, I'm not that stupid,' Carlotta retorted. 'I didn't know there were any keys in the locks. I haven't noticed any since I came on the yacht this time and I've never noticed them before. I've never wanted to lock myself in or to lock the doors when I've left the ship. I guess I've always felt safe on board with you and Jilly and the crew. I guess I've always felt I could trust you all.'

'Hmm.' Jilly had returned with a coffee-pot and was pouring the liquid into their mugs. 'Maybe you're too trusting, miss, she said, looking severe. 'Now I'm not saying that Stan or I or the crew can't be trusted. We can. But when we're tied up at a dock it's easy enough for any stranger to walk aboard without us seeing him or her. Unless we kept a member of the crew always posted at the gate we could be boarded at any time. I think you should always lock your cabin doors. Don't you, Stan?'

'Do you lock yours when you go ashore or when you go to bed at night?' asked Carlotta, raising her eyebrows at them and they both had the grace to look disconcerted.

'No, we don't, miss. But it might be a good idea if we all did,' said Stan Atkins. 'I should have suggested it to you when you arrived, but I just assumed you'd be careful and lock your doors always. There's been a lot of theft and piracy in the islands—not so much here on Morunda or on St Phipps where there's full employment, thanks to the tourist trade, but on some of the other islands where the economy isn't so well developed and there's a lot of poverty.'

'We've even heard of murders,' Jilly added. 'And we've heard of a crew and yacht we know being hi-jacked by four armed men in the island of the Dominican Republic. They were forced to take the men to Puerto Rico.'

'Did they get to Puerto Rico?'

'They had a bad crossing in the Mona Strait and everyone was ill,' the skipper took up the story. 'Then the engine quit. The armed men took to the Zodiac dinghy at that point because they were only a few hundred yards from the coast. They forgot about the radio. The crew of the yacht radioed the American coastguard and when the armed men went ashore they found a welcoming party of coastguards waiting for them.' He paused, and then added, 'That little escapade ended safely for the skipper and crew of the yacht. But it might not have done. I think it would be best if you locked your doors, miss.'

'Well, I will in future,' said Carlotta. 'But you haven't told me who locked my doors last night. Did you? Or did you give orders to the deckhand I met ashore last night to lock them?'

'Excuse me, now, miss,' he said politely, rising to his feet. 'Time I got back to the wheelhouse. We're just about to clear the harbour bar and I'd like to set the ship on course for St Phipps. See you later.'

He nodded at her, stood up, put on his cap and strode from the saloon. Alone, Carlotta sighed with frustration and drank some coffee. She was sure now that the skipper had instructed Brad to lock her in her cabin last night, and while she appreciated Stan Atkins's concern regarding the security of the yacht, it annoyed her when she realised she had been treated not as the adult woman she was but as if she were a troublesome, badly behaved adolescent given to staying out late at night and mixing with the wrong company. She was convinced now that the skipper must be acting on orders from her father.

When she had finished her breakfast Carlotta left the saloon and went aft to the sun-deck. There she leaned against the rail and looked about her. As the skipper had said, the *Montezuma* was crossing the bar of the harbour, rolling a little on the waves that surged across the long bank of sand and passing two tall ships anchored just inside the bar. One of them was a schooner and the other a Hermaphrodite brig. Carlotta knew they were both charter yachts that had sailed down from the Virgin Islands. The brig was making ready to set sail and she could see members of the crew up in the yards of its square-rigged foremast, unfurling a heavy sail.

Once over the bar the *Montezuma* changed course and turned to port. Its engines picked up speed as the yacht went south heading for another island, a series of pointed blue hills on the horizon.

Moving one of the loungers to face the sun, Carlotta lay down on it. She smoothed suntan oil on her arms and legs. She would have liked to sunbathe without her clothes on, but a certain consideration for the Atkinses, whom she suspected of being rather puritanical, prevented her from doing so. There would be chance enough for skinny-dipping and sunbathing naked on the beaches of St Phipps.

She lay back and closed her eyes behind the sunglasses. Down in the bowels of the yacht the engines throbbed regularly. The sun was hot and the air soft. She had all the time in the world to relax. There was nothing to bother her except the puzzle about who had actually turned the keys in the doors of her cabin last night.

She was glad they had left Morunda before Phillida Chalmers had come aboard for a visit. Now the embarrassment of having to tell Phillida the truth, admit to the older woman that Kurt was dead and that the man to whom she had been introduced last night was only a deckhand, could be postponed for a few days. She had time to think up some way of avoiding the embarrassment. Perhaps she could say that Kurt had gone away, returned to Europe. No, that wouldn't do because it was possible Phillida might see Brad on the yacht or even in the streets of Morrisburg. But she would think of something. Not right now. Tomorrow. *Mañana*. She smiled a little sadly to herself, thinking of her Spanish-American mother who had never done today what she could put off until tomorrow.

An hour later, alerted by the slowing down of the engines, she left the lounger and went up to the wheelhouse. The yacht was just entering a bay, skirting around some jagged-looking rocks against which water leapt up in fans of spray. Green and gold, covered by giant cacti and feathery-looking trees, two long headlands reached out, seeming to embrace the yacht, gathering it into the almost landlocked bay of

flat, silken water, so clear it was possible to see
fish darting about in the depths.

A hundred yards from the sun-shimmered
beach that rimmed the rocky land at the head of
the bay, the anchor was dropped and the engines
went into reverse. From the wheelhouse Carlotta
watched a deckhand move along the foredeck
below to the bow to check that the electronically
controlled anchor chain was running out freely.
The sun-bleached top strands of his dark hair
glinted and his body, bare to the waist, was
tanned to a ruddy brown. She felt a leap
of excitement as she recognised Brad, her
masquerade husband of the night before.

'That's Stenson Point over there.' Skip Atkins's
voice broke into her confused thoughts, and she
looked round to see him pointing to the green
headland on the right. 'If you look through the
glasses you'll see the stone jetty and a path
going through a plantation of palms. I suppose it
goes to the house. There's the jetty.'

Through the binoculars Carlotta surveyed the
jetty he had indicated, then turned so that she
could see the curve of the beach and the land
rising behind it. Another path was there, twisting
up to a road running along the ridge of land.
Her glance swept on along the road to a gate
and the other headland. Some Jersey cows grazed
the land behind a fence and there was a pen
with wire netting around it where white geese
waddled about. As she studied them a peacock
appeared and showed off its magnificent tail.
With a flutter of white wings, doves swooped up
and then down again.

Changing her stance, Carlotta trained the
binoculars on the only other boat in the bay. It

was a small sailing sloop, and sitting in the
cockpit were a young man and woman and a
blond-haired boy of about two. All were naked.
A faded French tricolour hung from the jackstaff
at the stern of the yacht. She felt sudden envy
of the couple, so contented in their own little
world of their boat with their baby. Then, aware
that she was prying into their privacy, she let
her glance swerve away from them and down to
the foredeck of the *Montezuma*.

Brad was still at the bow, leaning over the
side, checking the anchor, making sure it had
caught. He looked bigger and older than she
remembered, his shoulders very wide, his broad
back shimmering with muscle under his suntanned
skin. As she gazed at him, secretly admiring his
strong athletic body and long sinewy legs, he
moved, turned and looked up at the wheelhouse.
She saw the flash of his teeth as he smiled and
made a signal with one hand to the skipper, a
thumbs-up sign. The anchor was set. The engines
went into neutral and were turned off.

'I think I'll go ashore,' said Carlotta, putting
down the binoculars. She hoped Brad hadn't
noticed her staring at him through them. 'I'll
swim to the beach, take my snorkelling gear. I
won't go for long. I'll come back for lunch and
then later this afternoon someone could take me
over to Stenson Point in the launch.'

'You just please yourself, miss. As long as I
know where you've gone and where you'll be
going while we're anchored here, it's fine with
me.'

Fifteen minutes later, dressed in a sleek green
and white swimsuit, flippers on her feet and
snorkelling mask and tube in place, Carlotta

somersaulted into the clear water of the bay.
Soft and silken, it closed over her head as she
sank downwards. Swimming just below the
surface, she drifted slowly in the direction of the
beach. The bottom of the bay where the yacht
had anchored was covered with grass. She noted
that the anchor was firmly embedded in sand
just beyond the grass. There were no fish, no
coral heads, only smooth banks of golden sand
rippled by sunlight shining through the water.
She stood up. She was in about three feet of
water, and the beach was only a couple of strides
away.

The sun hot on her back and head, she waded
ashore. On the hill above her the geese protested
loudly, honking for all they were worth as they
sensed the presence of a stranger. A few palm
trees shaded the beach. She placed her flippers
and mask behind the trunk of one of them and
walked barefoot up a narrow path to the top of
the ridge. To her surprise the ridge was a narrow
isthmus of land between the Bay of Doves and
another bay on the side of the island that faced
south-east.

Turning, she looked back the way she had
come and felt another jolt of surprise. The beach
where she had come ashore was no longer empty.
A man was there. He was coming out of the
water just where she had waded out, and as she
watched him he sat down on the sand, as
she had done, to remove his flippers. Wide-
shouldered, lean-flanked, his skin the colour of
mahogany, she recognised him easily.

Had he followed her? Probably. Her lips
curled cynically. He probably wanted his US

dollars. Well, he wouldn't get them here. She hadn't brought her cheque book with her.

For a few moments she stood watching him, wondering if he would follow her up the path, but he didn't even look round to see where she was. He lay back on the sand, arms beneath his head.

Oh, well. Carlotta shrugged her shoulders. He hadn't followed her. It was his time off and he'd come ashore to be alone, to sunbathe and sleep perhaps. She turned away, crossed the narrow road that led up to the gate in a barbed-wire fence behind which the geese, the peacocks and a few cattle lived and began to clamber down the rocks to the narrow beach that rimmed the other bay. The geese honked and the peacock shrilled when they heard small stones clanging down the rocks, disturbed by her feet.

At last she reached the firm damp sand against which surf pounded. Exposed to the steady trade wind blowing straight off the Atlantic Ocean, water surged and foamed about numerous rocky islets in the bay.

She lingered at the edge of the beach, tempted to run out into the surf and ride the breakers as they charged in. Then, deciding there would be too many rocks lying beneath the surface for surfing to be any fun, she turned back wondering which was the best way to climb up to the road.

Her heart jumped. Brad was there, sitting among the rocks watching her. He was hardly discernible because he was sitting as still as any rock, his suntanned skin blending with their reddish brown colour, in the shade of a huge cactus.

Perhaps he thought she couldn't see him.

Mischief sparked through her. She would be revenged on him for giving her such a scare. She found a pebble and threw it in best baseball style. It struck a rock just to the right of him, quite close to his face. As she had hoped, it startled him. She saw his head move sharply as he glanced at the rock beside him. Then he looked back at her.

'Hi,' she called to him and waved an arm. 'Come down here. I want to speak to you.'

CHAPTER FOUR

THE man who was sitting so still on the rocks didn't move right away, and Carlotta wondered if he was going to ignore her imperious summons. Then slowly he stood up and began to step over the rocks. Like her he was barefoot but he moved more quickly than she had done, leaping with a catlike grace from one foothold to another, seeming to know instinctively where to find the right one.

When he reached the beach and came towards her Carlotta wished she hadn't asked him to come down. Naked except for his brief black swimming shorts, his sun-bronzed skin glowing in the sunlight, he presented a powerful sexuality that kept her gaze trapped on him. Conscious that her heart was beginning to beat much faster than usual and that her cheeks were unusually hot, she took in every detail of his muscular chest and shoulders, the bulge of biceps under the sleek skin of his upper arms, the strength of hairy forearms and finally the shapeliness of his long legs.

He was as lean and graceful as any jungle cat, yet older than she had guessed him to be the previous night. By the intermittent light of the patio, in the silvery radiance of the moon, she had judged him to be about twenty-nine or thirty. Now she could see he must be thirty-five, a strong attractive male in his prime.

And just as her glance seemed riveted to his masculine attractions his seemed caught and held by her feminine ones, drifting over her figure, golden-skinned and sleekly curvaceous in the close-fitting swimsuit.

On that crescent of yellow sand, beside the surging green foam-edged water, it was a meeting that vibrated with all kinds of sensual messages, and when he stopped before her, neither of them spoke for a few spellbound seconds. Speech didn't seem necessary.

Then, aware of the sun hot on one shoulder, burning through the oil on her skin, Carlotta stiffened, stepped back a pace and looked out at the bay, away from the mesmerising gaze of his dark eyes.

'I hope you haven't followed me ashore to get the money I owe you. I don't have my cheque book with me,' she murmured.

His eyebrows lifted a little, his lips curled in a slight smile.

'That isn't why I followed you,' he said, also speaking softly as if he had no wish to break the spell.

'Then you do admit you followed me just now, from the yacht?' she said quickly, looking straight at him again.

'Yes, I admit it.' He seemed to become aware that he was standing too close to her, and also stepped back a couple of paces, turning away from her to face the water, shading his eyes with one hand against the glare to look out at some sailing yachts beating past the entrance to the wide-open bay.

'Why? Why did you follow me if not for the money I owe you?' she demanded.

His hand dropped to his side and he turned back to face her again. His lean suntanned face was not easy to read and his dark eyes were shuttered.

'I followed you to keep an eye on you. To see that you don't do anything foolish like drowning or going off with strange men. It seems the last is a bad habit you have,' he said, his voice cool, a little scornful.

'Now just what do you mean by that?' she demanded covering her surprise with a show of haughtiness.

'You eloped with Kurt Malden. And then last night you picked me up in the marina bar.'

'I . . . I didn't pick you up,' she retorted angrily. 'I asked you to dance with me and to help me. But don't think for one minute that because we danced and I asked you to pretend to be my husband you have the right to follow me, or criticise me or to . . . to . . .'

'Take advantage of you?' he suggested smoothly with that annoying satirical flicker of his right eyebrow.

Her breath hissed between her teeth as she drew it in sharply to contain her irritation.

'Please go back to the yacht,' she ordered. 'I don't need your help any more and I don't need you to keep an eye on me. I'll give you a cheque for what I owe you as soon as I get back to the yacht. And that will be the end of it as far as I'm concerned.' She paused, frowning, remembering the number of times she had noticed him hovering near her in the town, in stores, in eating places, in discothèques. Had he been following her then? 'And please stop following me about,' she added.

'You don't owe me anything. Forget that,' he said coldly.

'But you said you wanted to be paid if you pretended to be Kurt. And I'd feel better if I paid you. I'd feel I'm not under an obligation to you for helping me. It . . . it was a wild impulse and . . . and——'

'And now you're regretting it.' He seemed to know how to express what she was feeling better than she did herself. 'I thought you might, and that's why I tried to put you off the idea by asking you how much you were prepared to pay me if I obliged by pretending to be Kurt.' Disgust grated in his voice and his lower lip curled. 'I thought the idea of me pretending to be your husband was crazy, a wild impulse, as you say, that needed to be nipped in the bud.'

'Then why did you say you were Kurt when Bernard asked who in hell you were?' She pounced sharply and felt a vague feeling of triumph when she saw she'd caught him off-guard.

Long fingers raked his hair. He frowned at the distant sailing yachts. The edges of white teeth chewed his lower lip.

'I hadn't reckoned on him being so bloody objectionable,' he growled, 'pushing between us the way he did.' His dark glance flicked back to her. 'But I didn't reckon either on you,' he continued his voice crisping, his face hardening. 'There was no way I could predict you'd introduce me to Mrs Chalmers as Kurt Malden. No way at all. It was you who tipped the fat in the fire. All I could think of to get us both out of an embarrassing situation was to ask Skip Atkins to leave the marina early this morning before Mrs Chalmers turned up and asked to see you and your husband.'

'Hey, wait a minute,' she cried out. 'Did you say *you* asked Skip Atkins to leave port this morning?'

'Yes, I did,' he admitted slowly, frowning again.

'But . . . but you're only a deckhand. You have no authority!' she spluttered. 'Why would Skip do what you ask him to do?'

The dark eyes considered her coolly. She felt as if she were being assessed for qualities she might not possess. The feeling unnerved her. Never had she been surveyed in such a way before. It was like having every defence stripped away and her soul laid bare for his inspection. She couldn't sustain his steady, penetrating gaze and looked away from him abruptly, tilting her chin.

'It's damned hot standing here,' he said at last. 'I wouldn't like either of us to get sunstroke. Supposing we find somewhere in the shade and I'll try to explain everything to you, why I've been following you, and why I have the authority to ask Skip Atkins to leave Morunda this morning. I'd hoped to do what I have to do without you knowing, but again I reckoned without you. I didn't know, you see, that you're given to wild impulses. Nor did I realise . . .' he paused and gave a self-mocking laugh, 'I hate to admit it,' he added, 'but I didn't count on you being so observant or so intelligent.'

Her head swung round. She gaped at him, her eyes opening wide.

'Whatever are you getting at?' she demanded huskily.

'I'll tell you when we're not being fried alive by the sun,' he replied, smiling a little. 'Come on, there should be some sort of shelter from it under the cliffs.'

He turned and began to walk along the beach. In puzzled bewilderment, obeying his order, she followed him. The beach became narrower where the cliffs advanced to the sea. A shallow cave opened up in the rock where the surf had eroded the foot of the cliff.

'How about this?' said Brad. 'Ideal for the purpose of a private conversation while the tide is out. Even some well-arranged rocks for us to sit on.'

Carlotta sat on one of the rocks but he sat on the damp sand. Stretching his long legs before him he leaned back on one elbow, supporting his head on his hand and looked out at the foaming, fretting water of the bay and the shimmering sails of the distant yachts.

'So. Begin. Explain,' ordered Carlotta imperiously, impatient with his silence.

He turned and looked at her, his dark glance raking her.

'Thank God, I'm not really your husband,' he drawled provocatively. 'I'm beginning to think Kurt had one hell of a time with you.'

'I can assure you Kurt gave far worse than he got,' she retorted. 'But we didn't come here to talk about him. What did you hope to do without me knowing or guessing?'

His eyes narrowed, grew wary again as he studied her face.

'To be your bodyguard,' he said quietly.

'My what?' She stared at him. 'But I don't need a bodyguard.'

'Mason J. Burr II,' he began—it seemed to give him some amusement saying her father's full name —'would disagree with you. He hired me to protect you, to go where you go.'

'Protect me from what?' She was indignant.

'From being kidnapped,' he said. His cheek bulged as he probed it with his tongue and the glance he gave from under his eyebrows mocked her. 'Could be he really wanted to prevent you from eloping again with an unsuitable suitor,' he added.

'But why should he think I'd be kidnapped?' she asked ignoring the jibe.

The mockery had gone from his face as if it had never flickered there. The glance he gave her now was serious.

'For some time, since you left Kurt Malden actually, your father has been receiving threatening letters. Anonymous letters. The writer of the letters has threatened to kidnap you and hold you to ransom if Mason J. Burr doesn't go along with his demands.'

'And those demands are?' she queried.

'The letters have been written apparently by someone who feels strongly about the treatment he has received from Burr-Tex oil company and requires recompense. If your father doesn't pay up, the writer threatens to kidnap you.'

'Oh, is that all?' she said with a sigh. 'He's been threatened like that before. People are always threatening to kidnap me, but I never have been, and Dad has never hired a bodyguard before. Why should he have hired one this time?'

'On the advice of his lawyer when he consulted him about the threatening letters,' Brad explained. 'The lawyer suggested that before any steps were taken to search for the writer of the letters someone should be hired to protect you. Since you were going to spend some time on the yacht, your father contacted Skip Atkins and asked him to find someone trained in security who could live on the yacht and keep an eye on you at the same time. Skip contacted me and I flew to Morunda to join the crew just before you arrived.'

'I see.' She was furious, made so by her father's behaviour in doing everything behind her back. 'Dad should have consulted me first,' she seethed. 'This is typical of his high-handed methods. I don't need a bodyguard. I hate being followed about and watched. I'm capable of looking after myself!'

'He doesn't think so, and you can hardly blame him, considering you eloped to marry someone he didn't approve of,' he sneered.

'How do you know he didn't approve of Kurt?' she demanded 'Did he tell you? Oh, I can't believe he would discuss me with . . . with someone he hired, with an employee.' Elbows on her knees she covered her hot cheeks with her hands. 'He had no right to. None at all——' she broke off, unable to express the emotional turmoil caused by the thought that her father could have betrayed her to a stranger.

'It's all right. He didn't discuss it with me. I just guessed,' Brad said softly. 'I didn't even know you'd eloped to marry Kurt until Mrs Chalmers mentioned that your marriage to him was "runaway". I'm sorry. I was out of line for saying what I did just now.'

She flashed a wide-eyed glance at him, encountered a warm, sympathetic expression in the dark eyes before they were veiled by thick, black lashes.

'What Dad didn't understand is that I wouldn't have eloped with Kurt if he hadn't been so critical of him or so over-protective of me,' she said more calmly, responding involuntarily to Brad's warm look. 'Dad's always been suspicious and jealous of any man I've dated. Always. He's presumed all of them to be fortune-hunters.'

'And wasn't Kurt a fortune-hunter?' he queried. He was playing with the sand, lifting a handful of it and letting it slide out through the spaces between his fingers, seeming to have lost interest in her again.

'I didn't think he was when I married him,' she admitted stiffly. 'But I still think Dad should have talked with me before he hired a bodyguard for me. It's time he stopped treating me as if I were a child.'

'Perhaps he would if you stopped behaving like one,' he suggested and the undercurrent of mockery was back in his voice.

'Oh, that's it!' She sprang to her feet. 'I don't have to sit here listening to criticism from you.'

'Sit down.' He was casual no longer. The order was rapped out sharply. 'I haven't finished explaining to you yet. If you stay and listen to me you might learn why your father didn't consult you before hiring me.'

'No. I won't sit down. I'm going right back to the yacht, I'm going to ask Skip Atkins to put through a ship-to-shore phone call to my father and I'm going to ask Dad to fire you. I don't want a bodyguard,' she stormed and began to stride past him.

Her ankle was caught by a big hand. Fingers of steel curled about its slenderness, threatening to crush the bones. She lost her balance and fell across his outstretched legs. All the breath was knocked out of her. For a few moments she lay there feeling his knees hard against her breasts. Then she felt his hand come down on her buttocks and she tensed all over. But the hand only slid rather caressingly over her smooth, rounded rump before being lifted away.

'I'm tempted,' he murmured, laughter shaking his voice. 'Very tempted. But no doubt you would sue me for assault or sexual harassment if I did, so I won't give you what you have probably never had from Mason J. Burr—and that is a good spanking.'

Gasping in outrage she thrust the heels of her palms against the sand and pushed herself away from him, rolling over to sit up, her legs curled under her. She was so angry she couldn't speak. She could only glare at him, her breasts rising and falling with barely controlled emotion. He looked back at her and began to laugh, his dark eyes crinkling at the corners, his teeth flashing white against the tan of his face, and unexpectedly his laughter hurt more than the spanking might have done.

'So what else do you have to explain?' she demanded haughtily.

He stopped laughing, drew his knees up and rested his arms on them. Once again his face was hard, almost grim, and his eyes were watchful.

'Just this. Your father guessed you would object to having a bodyguard if he consulted you, so we arranged that I should be hired as a deckhand as a cover for my activities.' He paused and looked down at the sand. 'I've followed you about for the past few weeks as unobtrusively as possible. I realise you've noticed me now and again and possibly wondered. It hasn't been easy keeping an eye on you, especially when you've visited a friend, gone into a house or aboard another yacht and I've had to hang around outside waiting for you to reappear. You also have a bad habit of staying out dancing until all hours of the morning. Lately I've been a bit short on sleep.'

'Really?' she found sufficient coolness to mock him in return. 'So why don't you give up? Tell my father you can't keep up with me? I'll be happy to be rid of you.'

His glance dismissed her suggestion scornfully.

'I don't give up,' he replied tautly. 'But this morning when Skip Atkins told me you were suspicious about having been locked in your cabin last night I decided to phone Mason J. Burr and ask his permission to tell you why he had hired me. After warning me you'd probably blow your top when you heard you had a bodyguard he gave me that permission. He knows you pretty well. He knows you're given to wild impulses and have spitfire qualities, contrary moods . . .'

'You're enjoying this, aren't you?' she hissed. 'You're taking a sadistic pleasure in pointing out the flaws in my character. Well, you'd better believe, Mr Bodyguard, that Dad was right. I object very much to having you around watching every move I make, trailing me through the streets of Morrisburg, locking me in my cabin so that you can snatch a few hours' sleep. And now I'm going to phone him, not to ask him to fire you but to tell him I've fired you myself!'

'You'll be wasting your time.' Twisting lithely to his feet at the same time as she stood up, he strode in front of her, blocking her escape from the cave.

Brawny forearms folded across his chest, six feet or more of compact bone and muscle, he towered over her, alert and ready to stop any move she might make to pass him.

'Your father won't fire me on your instructions and I won't leave the yacht or your side if you say you fire me. I was hired by him and I'll be fired by him only. Wherever you go I go until he says stop,' he said with a calm authority.

'You're very sure of yourself,' she countered, tilting her chin at him although she realised she had met her match. There was nothing she could do to get rid of him, at least, nothing she could think of right now.

'Always,' he said. 'I'm glad you've noticed.'

Her glance drifted down from his face over the strong column of his neck, the mat of crisp dark hair on his chest, his flat abdomen and further down to his thighs, straight legs and broad high-arched feet, and once again she felt the tingling pull of sexual attraction. He was different from any other man she had met. Quick-witted, coolly autocratic, he wasn't easily disconcerted and he seemed immune to her attractions, had made no attempt to capitalise on the kiss they had exchanged last night, to take the advantage she had feared he might take. He intrigued her, and she wanted suddenly to know more about him.

'Is your name really Brad?' she asked, looking up at him, with a mercurial change of mood. 'Is it your last name or your first name?'

Only the tell-tale quiver of his right eyebrow indicated that he might have been surprised by her change of attitude.

'It's a shortened version of my last name,' he said curtly.

'Bradley or Bradford or . . .?' She left the question hanging.

'Bradley.'

'And what's your first name?'

'Does it matter?' He was cool. 'You don't have to know. Brad is enough for you.'

'Oh, all right.' She shrugged. 'You're English, aren't you? Which part of England do you come from?'

'London. Does this catechism mean you've decided against phoning your father and asking him to dismiss me?'

'I guess it does.' She smiled at him, her best and most charming smile. 'I like to know something about a person I'm forced to associate with every day. Why did you lock me in my cabin last night?'

'I thought you knew. So I could snatch a few hours' sleep,' he retorted, his eyes glinting. 'To prevent you from going out again. Also to prevent anyone from walking into your cabin at night and kidnapping you. I removed the keys from the doors when I arrived on the yacht and I've locked you in after you've gone to bed ever since you came aboard.'

'Oh.' She had difficulty again in controlling a

quick spurt of anger. 'I wish you wouldn't. I hate being locked in or restrained in any way.' She drew a deep breath to control herself and gave him an up-from-under-look that should have melted his resistance to the appeal she was going to make. 'Now that I know you're my bodyguard and I'm aware of the possibility of being kidnapped will you please stop locking me in? I promise I won't go out at night without letting you know so you can come with me.'

'No.' Her efforts to charm him into relenting had had no effect. He was an immovable object standing there before her, arms folded, iron-hard, impregnable to the assault of feminine wiles. 'I'm still going to lock your doors. You'll get used to being locked in.'

'No, I won't. Never.' Her irritation with him flared out, a flame that should have scorched him but didn't.

'You would prefer to be kidnapped then and held to ransom? You want to put your father through hell worrying about you? Your mother too? Do you have no concern about the people who care about you? Care about what might happen to you?' he accused roughly.

'I don't have a mother. She died when I was sixteen,' she retorted, stung by his remarks. 'And I am concerned about my father. I don't want him to worry unduly about me. It's just that I don't like the idea of having a bodyguard.' Her breast rose and fell as she let out an exasperated sigh. 'Oh, I suppose I'll have to put up with it,' she grumbled sulkily.

'Growing up has always been a painful business,' he jibed. 'We all go through it. Shall we go back to the yacht now? It must be nearly lunchtime.'

'All right,' she agreed. 'But there is something else I ought to mention to you. I'm grateful to you for thinking up a way of us avoiding Phillida Chalmers today, but we've really only postponed the embarrassment of having her come to the marina and asking Skip Atkins if she can see me and my husband when we get back to Morunda. She stays on the island until the end of March.'

'Us? We?' His right eyebrow flickered. His eyes glinted with mockery. 'What's all this? You're talking as if we're partners in the crime of deception!'

'Well, aren't we? You went along with the idea. You didn't have to tell Bernard you were Kurt. You're just as responsible for deceiving him and Phillida as I am,' she retorted.

'That's true,' he conceded. 'I'll think of something during the next day or two while we cruise about the islands to get us out of our masquerade marriage, to divorce us from one another. Don't you worry about it!'

'But you'll tell me, won't you? What you think of?' she said urgently, following him as he walked to the entrance of the cave. 'I'll have to know what you're going to do or even say if we run into Phillida again, so that I don't foul everything up.'

'I'll try to warn you. If there is time and it's necessary,' he replied coolly. 'Now, would you mind if we return to the yacht? I'm ready for my lunch, but until you decide to go back I'll have to stay with you—at a distance, of course, suppressing the pangs of my hunger.' He smiled at her, his eyes dancing with amusement. 'You see how my life is governed by every wild whim of yours. No longer am I my own master.'

His mockery of the situation between them, she as the person who needed protection and he as her protector, struck a chord in her and she laughed, feeling again a strong pull of attraction and they walked along the beach side by side, in a strange but silent communion, as if they knew each other well, as if they were partners, not in crime but in adventure, the adventure of life. As if . . . the thought sidled stealthily and almost unnoticed into Carlotta's mind . . . as if they really were married.

CHAPTER FIVE

ACROSS the road and down the path under the few palms, Carlotta followed Brad to the beach in the Bay of Doves. Under the soles of her bare feet the sand was burning hot and the glare of light on the water was hurtful to the eyes. She searched for and found her flippers and snorkelling mask, and she was just going to join Brad at the edge of the beach, where he was sitting to pull on his flippers, when she heard a high, shrill voice calling her name. Looking round, she saw a woman running towards her, floundering in the soft sand. Behind the woman, drawn up on the beach, was the red Zodiac dinghy she had noticed moored at the jetty below Stenson Point. Suddenly she recognised the running woman and, dropping her snorkelling gear, set off to meet her.

Arms reaching out to each other they met and embraced warmly.

'Tizzy, it's great to see you,' Carlotta exclaimed. 'I was hoping you might be staying at the house. I was going to come over later.'

'It's great to see you, too.' Tizzy was out of breath and her wide grin almost split her thin triangular face in half. As usual her mop of light brown, gold-tipped curls was in an unkempt tangle falling to her shoulders. 'I recognised the

Monte so I went over to see if you or your dad
were on board. The captain said you were here
on the beach.' She looked past Carlotta, her
sparkling grey eyes opening wide. 'Oh, land's
sakes,' she breathed in her Texan drawl. 'Who's
with you, Carlo? He's super, absolutely super!
Trust you to grab the cream of the crop!' Tizzy
slapped a hand against her brow as if smitten by
a sudden, enlightening thought. 'But of course,
you're married now, aren't you?'

Before Carlotta could do or say anything Tizzy
launched herself forward, holding out her right
hand. Turning, Carlotta saw that Brad had come
up behind her.

'Hi,' Tizzy greeted him. 'I'm Teresa Carter
and I've known Carlo for years. You must be
her husband. What shall I call you?'

'He isn't . . .' Carlotta was beginning when a
swift sharp glance from Brad silenced her.

'I'm Kurt Malden,' he said taking Tizzy's hand
in his, smiling down at her. 'And what shall I
call you?'

'You can call me Tizzy, everyone does. I guess
it's because I'm usually in a tizzy about something
and right now it's about meeting Carlo and you
right here, on this beach!' She gazed up at him
and gave a sigh. 'You wouldn't have any
brothers, would you?' she went on. 'One between
twenty-six and thirty would do. I'm willing to fly
over to Europe to meet him.'

'Tizzy, shut up,' snapped Carlotta. The
strangest feelings were swirling through her. She
didn't like the way Tizzy was hanging on to
Brad's hand or the way she was looking up to
him. She didn't like the way he was smiling at

Tizzy either and making no attempt to let go of Tizzy's hand. 'You'll embarrass Kurt . . .'

'Sorry, Tizzy. No brothers,' said Brad. To Carlotta's further irritation, he didn't seem at all embarrassed by her friend's brash manner. Then he seemed suddenly to remember he was playing a part, and glanced quickly and enquiringly at Carlotta. Frowning, she shook her head at him, trying to convey that she didn't approve of his behaviour at the same time as letting him know that Kurt hadn't had any brothers.

'That's a pity,' moaned Tizzy, then abruptly abandoned the game of flirting with Brad. Letting go of his hand at last, she turned to Carlotta. 'Ethan's at the house,' she went on, adding for Brad's information, 'he's my brother, and he used to be Carlotta's best beau!

'Tizzy, that was years ago!' Carlotta interrupted sharply. 'It was over long before I went to Europe.'

'It isn't over for Ethan,' asserted Tizzy rather fiercely. 'You'll come up to the house, both of you, to see him, won't you? You see, he can't come to see you, Carlo. Since that plane crash he was in he hasn't been able to walk.'

'Ethan can't walk? I didn't know the accident was that bad,' whispered Carlotta, feeling chilled in spite of the hot sun.

'It's a sort of paralysis caused by a pinched nerve in his spine,' explained Tizzy, serious now, her bright eyes clouded with sadness. 'It's been awful for him, Carlo, but I know he'll cheer up when he knows you're here. Come over now, come for lunch. You too, Kurt.'

'Thank you for the invitation,' Brad said, 'but I would prefer to go back to the yacht for lunch.

Perhaps we could come later, when it's getting cooler.'

'Great.' Tizzy perked up again. 'Come around five for drinks and stay for supper. That OK with you, Carlo?'

'I guess so.' Carlotta couldn't help being truculent. As soon as they got back to the yacht she would have a few plain words with Brad. He was assuming far too much. He was assuming he could decline or accept invitations on her behalf.

'So I'll take you back to the yacht now in the Red Monster,' said Tizzy lightly. 'Come on, Kurt, and help me push off.'

On the deck of the *Montezuma*, after she had climbed up the ladder and Tizzy had zoomed off in the direction of Stenson's Point, Carlotta turned on Brad.

'I don't really want to deceive Tizzy,' she complained. 'I'd have told her you aren't my husband if either of you had given me half a chance. She's been my friend for the longest time and I've never lied to her.'

'How was I to know that?' he retorted coolly. 'I thought you'd had time to explain to her who I was.'

'She . . . she jumped to a conclusion before I could say anything. She knew I'd married and she . . . just assumed you were Kurt. She's like that.'

'Another little rich girl who doesn't think before she acts or speaks,' he jeered nastily. 'Well, the damage is done now, and it might be a good idea to keep up the pretence.'

'But I don't want to,' she stamped one bare foot on the deck. 'I'm going to tell her the truth when I go ashore tonight. I'm going to tell her you're my bodyguard. I'm going to tell Ethan, too.'

His eyes narrowed dangerously and his lips tightened.

'I wish now I'd given you that spanking. Talk about contrary and headstrong,' he said and stepped closer to her, overpowering her with his superior height and heavy muscular shoulders. 'Now, listen to me, princess. We're having no more wild impulses. When we go ashore—I say we because I have to go with you as your bodyguard if not as your pretence husband— you'll say nothing to Tizzy or to Ethan until I give you permission to do so. You'll wait until I've checked out the other people at the house. There could be guests staying with the Carters, people you don't know and have never met before, even your kidnapper could be there. You'll keep your mouth shut and allow Tizzy to introduce us as Carlotta and Kurt Malden. I don't want it broadcast through the social élite of these islands that I'm your bodyguard. The fewer the people who know that the better. Once I've sized up the situation over there I'll let you know if it will be all right to tell your friends the truth. Got it?'

'Supposing I don't get it,' she fumed. 'Supposing I blurt out the truth to Tizzy as soon as we arrive? What will you do?'

'If that's going to be your attitude I'm going right now to tell the skipper to weigh anchor and leave this place because I don't consider it safe for you to be here,' he said grimly and, stepping round her, made for the steps going up to the wheelhouse.

'Oh, no.' She hurried after him. 'No. I don't

want to leave. I want to go ashore. I want to see Ethan. I promised I'd go. Please, Brad, don't tell Skip Atkins to leave.'

He turned slowly to face her, eyes still narrow, his expression hard and unrelenting.

'If you want to see Ethan you'll stay with the masquerade for a while. If you say one word to Tizzy or Ethan about our pretence without my agreement I'll make you look such a fool you'll be sorry you ever opened your mouth,' he threatened.

'I hate you,' she flung at him, not able to think of any other wounding remark.

'Because you can't get the better of me?' he suggested, 'Or because you're hoping to revive your old romance with Ethan Carter and that will be difficult to do with your husband in attendance?'

'That never entered my mind.' She was wincing from his jeering jibe. 'I just want to see Ethan, talk to him. Oh, all right.' She gave in suddenly as he began to head for the stairs again. 'I won't say anything to him or to Tizzy until you say I can.' She tilted her chin at him, and dropped her eyelashes, trying to achieve a supercilious pose. 'I'll meet you here around four thirty, and don't keep me waiting.'

'And between now and then?' he asked.

'Do I have to tell you everything?' she exploded.

'Just give me some idea of where you'll be. You must see I have to know where you are to be able to protect you,' he replied reasonably.

'After a lunch I'll go to my cabin to rest—but you needn't lock the doors,' she retorted snappily and went into the saloon.

Carlotta lunched alone on conch salad, a banana and ice-cold lemonade. In her cabin she lolled on her bunk, enjoying the pleasant coolness provided by the yacht's air-conditioning. She tried to read the latest bestseller but found the adventures of the liberated woman who was the heroine of the novel less interesting than her own, so she tossed it aside. Curling up, she closed her eyes hoping to doze as she often did in the heat of the tropical afternoons, instinctively following the habit of *siesta* inherited from her mother.

But, annoyingly, her brain was too active for dozing. It buzzed with all sorts of questions and images. She thought of the threatening letters her father had received and wondered who had sent them. She regretted the lack of communication between herself and her father, which she had increased and widened by her own wayward behaviour. Contrary, headstrong, Brad had called her and he was right, damn him. She was. Or she had been.

Images of Brad crowded into her mind, pushing out thoughts of her father. She saw him as he had been last night, sitting at a table on the patio at the marina. He had attracted her then. Why? Because he had seemed so indifferent to her? She had been the only other person on the patio yet he hadn't glanced at her once, or so she had thought.

The picture changed. She saw him as he had been today, wearing only brief swimming shorts, his suntanned skin glowing, his dark eyes slanting narrow, dangerous glances at her, and her pulses leapt as she felt the tug of his attraction. Better be careful. Once Kurt had attracted her, and look what had happened!

Rolling on to her other side she tried to obliterate Brad with an image of Ethan Carter, but Ethan wouldn't appear. For some reason she had almost forgotten what he looked like. Brad slid before her mind's eye again, dark eyes looking at her now with that hint of sympathy in their depths. As if he cared about her, as if he understood her.

She must stop thinking about him. He was her bodyguard, not her lover, but he was a bodyguard who was her partner in a dangerous deception, pretending to be her husband . . . Her pulses leapt suddenly as she imagined how he might behave if he was really her husband. He would kiss her as he had kissed her last night.

She slipped into a doze imagining she was in Brad's arms being kissed and didn't waken until she heard a knock on the door.

'Come in,' she called, sitting up and swinging her legs over the edge of the bunk.

Jilly entered the cabin carrying a tray set with teacups and a teapot.

'I've just made myself a pot of tea and I thought you might like some,' she said brightly. 'I know it isn't what you Yanks go in for . . .'

'But I'm not a Yankee,' Carlotta interrupted her quickly. 'I'm a Southerner, and I'd love a cup of tea. My grandmother Burr is English, too, and she always has tea in the afternoon, so I'm used to it. Sit down and we'll have a gossip. You can tell me something about Brad.'

Jilly looked up from pouring tea, her grey eyes wary.

'What do you want to know about him?' she asked.

'It's all right. I know why he's with us. He told me when we went ashore why my father has hired him as my bodyguard,' said Carlotta. 'All I want to know is what you know about him. Where and when did you and Skip meet Brad?'

'When we were in the Bahamas, last winter,' replied Jilly. She handed Carlotta a cup of tea with a slice of lemon and took her own cup over to the settee berth on the other side of the cabin from the bunk bed. 'We cruised the Bahamas with your father, your stepmother and your grandmother, so I do know what you're talking about when you say she sticks to her English habits and likes afternoon tea. She's such a sweet lady. She told me she met your grandfather when he was visiting England once. I suppose you have English cousins?'

'Yes. In Berkshire.' Carlotta squeezed lemon into the tea. 'But about Brad,' she prompted.

'Oh, yes. Well, as I was saying, Stan and I met Brad when we were in Nassau. He was living and working there. We brought him on board and he met your father. He told us he was working as a consultant to the Bahamian government, helping to organise a security force to deal with drug-traffickers and terrorists.' Jilly sipped some of her tea. 'He's well qualified to do a security job. He's been with Scotland Yard for years.'

'You mean he's a cop?' exclaimed Carlotta.

'Yes. Or he was. He was in the Yard's D 11 unit for a while. They're a tough lot from all accounts, and are usually called out to guard airports or embassies or government offices when there's been any terrorist threat. He has a desk job now, planning and organising.' Jilly looked suddenly anxious. 'I hope you're not upset, miss, at finding out he's your bodyguard. I'm sure you'll find he's good at it, a real professional.'

'Mmm. I suppose he is,' murmured Carlotta. 'I've never known a cop before.'

'Nor have I,' said Jilly, relaxing again. 'And I wouldn't have guessed Brad was a cop when Stan and I first met him. We were in the casino on Paradise Island, having a flutter at the tables one night and he was right next to us, having his fling too, same as anyone else, betting and losing. He dances well, too. We went to a discothèque with him afterwards and I danced with him. Stan won't dance. Doesn't like rock and roll and that stuff, he says. Is that all you want to know about Brad?'

'Is that all you know?'

'Well, yes, it is really. I can only add that his parents live in Cornwall, his father retired a couple of years ago, and he hasn't been married.' Jilly looked anxious again. 'I hope you're satisfied with him, miss, because Stan and I are right glad your father hired him. We feel less worried about you now that there's someone on board properly trained to keep a look out for would-be muggers or kidnappers. And I'm really glad Brad has told you himself why he's been hired. To tell the truth, I thought it was daft not telling you that he's here to protect you.'

'I guess Dad had good reason for not telling me,' said Carlotta with a touch of irony. 'And yes, I'm satisfied with what you've told me about Brad. I was a bit miffed when I found out why he's been hired but I've calmed down now. He'll be going ashore with me to my friend's house on the island this evening, so neither of us will be wanting dinner, Jilly. We'll come back around eleven, I guess. You might tell Skip.'

'I will,' promised Jilly, getting to her feet. 'Finished your tea?'

'Yes, thanks. It was great. Hit the spot. And thanks again for the information about Brad.'

'You're welcome. I'm sure you'll feel a lot safer with him around,' said Jilly, as she picked up the tray. 'We're all here to do our best for you, miss,' she went on a little diffidently. 'Your father intimated that you'd had a bad time of it lately and that we were to make sure everything went smoothly for you until he's able to join you. I hope you enjoy your visit ashore.'

'I hope so, too,' murmured Carlotta as she pushed open the door so that Jilly could leave.

She spent the next hour choosing the clothes she would go ashore in, showering again and then dressing and doing her hair. Black pants, silky and full, like those worn by eastern belly-dancers. A long tunic created from emerald silk tussore which she clinched at her waist with a gold lamé belt. She wound her hair up into a french pleat at the back of her head and frothed out the shorter strands in front to fall over her brow. With her eyes made up and her full lips red as poppies she thought she looked sultry and seductive. Would she seem like that to Brad, she wondered? And was surprised again by that leap of her pulses at the thought of meeting him and going into the Carter house with him at her elbow posing as her husband.

He was ready and waiting for her at the gate in the yacht's rail. He was wearing another lightweight white suit, this time with a dark red shirt open at the neck. After one glance at her, an all-seeing glance that swept her appearance from head to toe, he went down the ladder to the yacht's tender that was bobbing on the water. She followed him, going down the ladder backwards and felt his hand take her arm to steady her when she left the ladder to step down into the sleek white speedboat.

The sun had begun its swift slide down to the western horizon and the bay was filled with golden light. On the Point of Doves the rocks glowed purple and red and above them the rough vegetation covering the headland shimmered bright green and yellow against the pale duck-egg blue of the eastern sky. Yet the jetty that jutted out from Stenson Point lay in the shadow cast by the bulk of that headland. Tiny lizards scurried out of the way as Carlotta walked along the path that twisted up from the jetty through a plantation of palms, and the heavy drooping fringes of the leaves rustled and creaked in the light evening breeze that had sprung up.

Although there was room for them to walk side by side along the path, Brad walked behind her which began to irritate her before they had gone too far. Abruptly she stopped walking and turned to face him. He was forced to stop too or collide with her. Jacket pushed back by his arms, hands thrust into his trouser pockets he looked at her without expression, his eyes darker than ever in the shadows. She waited for him to ask her why she had stopped but he said nothing, just stood there surveying her with indifference, she thought, and that annoyed her even more.

'Jilly tells me you used to be a cop with Scotland Yard,' she said curtly.

'I thought you'd be checking up on me,' he replied, the line of his mouth relaxing a little. 'And I'm glad you did. It doesn't do to accept anyone at face value, in your position. It's best to be suspicious of strangers. I'd guess you've never been suspicious of anyone in your life and have trusted everyone.'

'Meaning, I suppose, that I'm naïve and easily taken for a ride,' she retorted icily. 'Another quality I possess that you don't approve of, like my contrariness and impulsiveness.'

'I never said I don't approve of you,' he replied calmly. 'I just pointed out that being the way you are makes it difficult for me—or anyone else—to protect you from harm.' He glanced into the shadows of the trees, then looked back at her. 'So did Jilly satisfy you about my qualification for this job of being your bodyguard?' he asked.

'Oh, Jilly is most impressed by you. She says you must be a tough guy because you were once a member of an élite security team. Do you carry a gun?'

'Sometimes.'

'Now?'

'No.'

'Why not? How will you deal with anyone who tries to kidnap me?'

'There are other ways. Using a gun is a last resort.'

'I see.' With a sudden swing of mood, feeling a sudden and mischievous desire to make him like her, she smiled at him. 'OK, now that I've checked you out and have found out you're a real professional, why don't we walk on together, arm in arm? We are pretending to be married, remember?'

His face froze. He gave her a dark inimical glance.

'Plenty of time for that when we get nearer to the house and might be observed by your friends and their guests,' he said coolly. 'Right now I'd prefer to walk behind you. Then no one can come up on you from behind or from out of the trees without me seeing him or her.'

'Oh.' Chilled as much by his refusal to respond to her smile as by his suggestion that she might be exposed to danger even here on this island, she turned and walked on.

Soon the path gave a final twist and they arrived at stone gateposts. A wide road curved off to the left. Inside the gateposts they followed a driveway between flower beds crammed with blossoming tropical shrubs and shaded by ornamental trees. Ahead of them a whitewashed house with a red-tiled roof glimmered in the fast-falling dusk. A long deck built out from the front of the house and festooned with coloured lights and delicate creeping plants was crowded with people, talking and laughing.

Brad advanced to her side and she felt his hand cup her elbow. A strange shiver compounded of distaste and delight shook her at his touch: dislike because he was a man and touching her, delight because it was Brad touching her.

'Time now for the arm-in-arm bit,' he murmured, letting go of her elbow and lifting her right hand through the crook of his left arm. 'Now we're all set. Do you think we look as if we're married?' Mockery rippled through his voice.

She was unable to respond this time to his mockery in any way. They were fast approaching the wide, shallow steps that led up to the long, covered deck. Tizzy, spotting them, rushed towards them.

'Carlo, so glad you've come!' she exclaimed, and Carlotta, with a new and sharp observation for detail, noticed that Tizzy hardly glanced at her, even though she greeted her hospitably. The gaze of her friend's grey eyes was directed at Brad, and that gaze was boldly admiring, openly flirtatious. Carlotta felt a sort of sickness rising within her. For the first time in all the years she had known Tizzy she felt an unreasonable envy of her, an irritation with her that twitched and niggled somewhere in the region of her stomach.

'Glad you've come too, Kurt,' Tizzy breathed. 'You're *most* welcome.'

Stop it, Tizzy. Stop making eyes at him. Carlotta bit hard into her lower lip so that she wouldn't scream at her friend as Tizzy tucked a hand through the crook of Brad's right arm.

'Come on, Kurt, I'll introduce you to everyone,' Tizzy said. 'Carlotta knows most of the crowd. Ethan is over there, Carlo, by the trellis, in his wheelchair. He's just dying to see you, so go and speak to him right away while I take care of Kurt.'

To Carlotta's secret annoyance Brad's arm dropped away from hers and he went off with Tizzy without a word or a glance. For a moment she stood alone on the edge of the group of guests, feeling deserted and thinking to herself

that Brad was a fine bodyguard, going off with
her best friend and leaving her exposed to
danger.

But she wasn't alone for long. Tizzy's mother,
small and blonde, bright as a bird, came up to
her.

'Carlo, it's great to see you again.'

Ali Carter's thin arms embraced her and she
was kissed on both cheeks.

'Only the other day we were having dinner
with Mason and Cora and he was telling us you
were down here, staying on the yacht. We were
hoping we'd run into you. Tizzy tells me your
husband is with you and that he's absolutely
gorgeous,' babbled Ali in her scatterbrained way.
Then with a glisten of tears in her eyes she
whispered. 'Ethan was really badly knocked
when he heard you had married. Poor boy.
You'll be kind to him, Carlo, please. He's had a
lousy time of it lately, with the plane crash and
all.'

'Tizzy says he can't walk,' whispered Carlotta,
allowing Ali to take her hand and lead her
through the guests to a far corner of the deck
festooned with blossoming vines.

'He *can* walk,' Ali replied. 'But not very well,
and we're having a hell of a time getting him to
exercise to strengthen his muscles. I'm warning
you, Carlo, he isn't like he used to be. He's lost
his zest for life, but I'm hoping the sight of you
will recharge his batteries. Now, what's the
matter? Who are you looking for?'

Carlotta had stopped, pulled her hand from
Ali's grasp and was looking for Brad. He wasn't
far away and was being introduced to Caldwell
Carter, Tizzy's father.

'I'd like Kurt to meet Ethan,' she said.

'But not right now,' said Ali. 'Later, when you and Ethan have had a little talk.' She took Carlotta's hand again and pulled her forward. 'Hey, Ethan' she called out. 'Look who's here!'

CHAPTER SIX

THE young man of her own age, whose hair was the same ripe wheat colour as her own but whose eyes were a brilliant blue like his mother's, made a supreme effort when she approached him and stood up.

Secretly shocked by his thinness and by the lines suffering had carved in his once-cheerful face, Carlotta dropped her new-found and hard-won reserve, went up to him and flung her arms around him. Tears sprang in her eyes as she realised how badly injured this friend of her childhood and youth had been when he had crashed his light plane. She kissed his cheek and he turned his head quickly to kiss her lips. Then with a little laugh he sat down abruptly in the wheelchair.

'Sorry about that, Carlo,' he said. Reaching forward he caught both her hands in his. 'They give way suddenly. The legs, I mean. Come and sit down. On that chair. Tizzy had it put there specially for you.'

She sat on the edge of the elegant deckchair, her hands still trapped in his.

'Ethan, oh, Ethan, what did you do to yourself?' she whispered.

'I'm not sure what happened. Engine cut out and the plane went into a nose-dive. Next thing

I knew I was in hospital hooked up to all kinds of life-support systems. But what about you? What in hell happened to you? Why did you get married the way you did? We all got the impression the other night your dad wasn't too pleased about your marriage.'

She looked down at their entwined hands rather than face the directness of his blue stare. The urge to tell him that she had made a terrible mistake in marrying Kurt and that her husband was no longer alive was very strong, but she had to contain it until Brad gave her permission to tell her friends the truth.

'I suppose you did it in one of your rebellious moods,' said Ethan. She looked at him. He was watching her closely.

'Guess I did,' she laughed lightly. 'You know me, Ethan. As soon as anyone tells me not to do something I do it. Dad showed his distrust and dislike of Kurt, so of course I immediately wanted to marry him.'

'And now you're regretting it?' he suggested, leaning towards her, his face close to hers.

'Yes, I am,' she admitted and moved back from him a little, but too late, she noticed with a sudden flushing of her cheeks when she looked round. Tizzy was approaching with Brad. They were holding hands.

'Ethan. This is Kurt, Carlo's husband,' Tizzy sang out. Still holding Brad's hand, she looked tiny beside the tall, rugged security man. She was a miniature but very pretty woman, natural-looking with untidy hair and wearing a multi-coloured silk dress. Looking at her friend, Carlotta felt suddenly too tall, too leggy in her baggy pants, too made-up, too much the sultry seducer, and wished she too had worn a dress and had tried to look more naturally feminine. Maybe Brad would have looked at her as he was looking at Tizzy, with a sort of affectionate appreciation. Jealousy of Tizzy exploded within her unexpectedly.

'Glad to meet you, Kurt.' Ethan's greeting of her counterfeit husband betrayed nothing of his knowledge that she was regretting her marriage. He held out his right hand and Brad shook it and murmured something appropriate.

'We're all going to eat now,' said Tizzy. 'Food is set out inside. But you two stay here and we'll bring you some, won't we, Kurt?'

They started to move away. Pulling her hands out of Ethan's, Carlotta sprang to her feet and went after them without giving any excuse to Ethan.

'Kurt, wait,' she said imperiously as she caught up with Brad and Tizzy at the archway. She saw Brad's shoulders stiffen and his head go up. He turned to face her. Shadows from hanging plants dappled his face, making his expression unreadable, but she had the impression the gaze of the dark eyes was cold and hostile. It was difficult to convey a message to him with Tizzy hovering at his elbow.

More than irritated with her best friend's behaviour—it seemed to her that Tizzy was getting possessive about Brad—Carlotta went right up to him, smiling at him. She put a hand on his chest and looked up at him from beneath her long black lashes and fine, arching eyebrows, her long fingers playing with a lapel of his jacket.

'Darling,' she murmured, but loud enough for Tizzy to hear. 'I'd like a word with you.' She shot a glance at the bright-eyed, inquisitive Tizzy. 'In private,' she added meaningfully.

'But of course.' He played up beautifully. 'Excuse us, Tizzy. I'll come in a few moments to choose food for myself and Carlotta. Now, what is it, sweetheart?' A glint of mockery danced briefly in his eyes and as he lifted her hand from his chest he carried it to his lips and kissed the back of it. Out of the corners of her eyes Carlotta saw Tizzy frown and turn away sharply to go into the house. Immediately Carlotta tried to pull her hand from Brad's grasp but his fingers tightened.

'She's gone,' she whispered. 'You can stop play-acting now.'

'Maybe I'm not acting,' he retorted, smiling at her. 'And there is someone else watching from his corner. Your erstwhile best beau.' He seemed amused by that description of Ethan. 'What is it you want to say to me in private? I guess this is as private as we'll get unless we leave. And you won't want to do that yet. Nor do I. I've seen the food that's spread out inside.'

She did want to leave, she realised. She wanted to give in to the jealous rage that was flaming inside her and drag him away with her, away from Tizzy. She wanted to behave as she would have done if he had really been her husband.

'I . . . I just want to say . . .' She broke off confusedly as the line from Stevie Wonder's hit number jingled through her mind. The next words were *I love you*. She drew a hissing breath. 'To tell you I can't understand your behaviour,' she continued shakily. 'You're suppo-sed to be protecting me. I don't understand how you can do that if you go off with Tizzy and leave me on my own . . .'

'But you weren't entirely alone,' he interrupted smoothly. 'You were with Ethan, quite safe, I would have thought.' He stepped closer to her. To anyone watching they must look like a very loving couple, her hand in his, their heads touching. 'I've had a good look at everyone here. I don't think any of them are kidnappers. They're a well-heeled lot, drawing wealth from oil companies, I shouldn't wonder.' Dryness rasped in his voice. 'Not the types to stoop to criminal activities such as blackmail or kidnapping. Go back now to Ethan and I'll fetch you some food. I won't be long.'

To her surprise he dropped a light kiss on her temple and squeezed her hand before releasing it and, while she was still feeling surprise, he left her, to saunter, hands in pockets, through an archway into the house.

'Carlo, come back.' Behind her, Ethan called to her and turning slowly she went over to him and sank down on to the chair beside him. 'Judging by appearances only he seems a nice guy,' he said. 'So why are you regretting having married him?'

'Mmm?' She was still watching the archway through which Brad had gone and wondering just what he was doing in there while he chose food. Was Tizzy with him, nudging against him, making up to him, making him laugh? So engrossed in imagining what they were doing together, she didn't hear Ethan's question. 'What did you say?' Dragging her gaze away from the archway she forced herself to attend to him.

'I said, he seems a nice guy, so why are you

regretting having married him?' The blue eyes
regarding her held a puzzled expression.

'Oh, did I say that? What I meant was I'm
regretting the way in which we eloped. I didn't
realise Dad would be so angry about it. I wish
now we'd waited, done it properly,' she said.

'Then there's no chance of you splitting up?'
said Ethan looking even more puzzled.

'Splitting up? You mean, is our marriage on
the rocks?' she asked.

'Guess I do. You see, Carlo, when he was
with us last week, before we flew out here, your
dad gave us to understand that . . . well, that
you had left Kurt already, and . . .'

'Oh, I had,' she replied a little wildly. 'But
he . . . he followed me.' So why hadn't she
asked Brad just now if she could confide in
Ethan, tell him the truth? Because she hadn't
wanted to, because she had wanted to continue
with the pretence that he was her husband. She
didn't want Tizzy in particular to know the truth.
She didn't want Tizzy to feel free to pursue
Brad and grab him for herself. She smiled at
Ethan, serenely, she hoped. 'We've made it up,'
she said. 'We're reconciled. It was only a little
tiff, the sort married couples have. Now we're
together again . . .' She broke off in amazement
at herself. What the hell was she going on like
this for? What had happened to the urge to tell
Ethan the truth? She decided to change the
course of the conversation. 'But what about you,
Ethan? Ali was just telling me you won't exercise
and won't try to walk. Why not? What's
happened to the gutsy guy I used to know?
Don't tell me that a little accident with a plane
has turned you into a chicken?'

'A little accident?' Ethan began to object, his eyes flashing angrily. 'If you knew the agony, the pain——' He broke off and began to laugh. 'Oh, Carlo,' he said. 'You're just what I needed! How like you to accuse me of lacking guts instead of soft-soaping me with too much sympathy. You're right. I have turned into a chicken, afraid to walk in case walking hurts too much.' He leaned towards her. 'I wish to hell you hadn't married Kurt,' he whispered. 'I wish you'd leave him again or tell him to get lost. I want you, Carlo. I always have. You're my best girl. I had it all planned. I was going to ask you to marry me when you came back from Europe. But you didn't come back, and I crashed my plane so I couldn't come after you.'

Carlotta stared at him in silence, trying to analyse her feelings where he was concerned. She didn't love him, she knew that, had decided she didn't before she had gone to Europe. If he had followed her to Europe and had asked her to marry him she would have refused him. He was her friend just as Tizzy was, but she could never have considered him as a lover.

'I'm sorry, Ethan. I . . . I didn't know you felt like that about me,' she muttered and with a sense of relief saw Brad approaching carrying a tray on which there were plates of food. Behind him came Tizzy.

But Brad and Tizzy, after bringing food to her and Ethan, didn't stay to eat with them. They went back into the house.

'You don't mind lending Kurt to me for a while, do you?' Tizzy said lightly to Carlotta. 'There's something wrong with the stereo system and he says he can fix it. We all want to dance after we've eaten. What's the good of a party if we can't dance?'

Carlotta watched them going wishing she could follow. She did mind lending Brad to Tizzy although she knew she wouldn't have objected to lending Kurt, she thought irritably. What in hell's name was wrong with her? Why get mad just because the guy who had been hired as her bodyguard seem to prefer to be with Tizzy than with her? She had Ethan, didn't she? But she didn't want Ethan. She wanted Brad. The truth seemed to come up out of nowhere and land her a punch in the solar plexus. She gasped. Ethan looked at her sharply and she covered up quickly.

'Hiccups,' she explained. 'I always did eat too quickly. Can I get you more?' She held out a hand for his empty plate.

'I'll come with you,' he said, surprising her, and began to pull himself to his feet. 'Just to show you I'm not chicken!' he said with a grin.

Supporting himself on two aluminium sticks, he walked slowly and with obvious painful effort into the house with her. As they entered the low-ceilinged, wide room where a long table was set with bowls and dishes of food, Ali saw them and came over to them.

'Good,' she said to her son. 'I guess if anyone could get you to move it would be Carlo.' She leaned forward until she could whisper in Carlo's right ear. 'Tizzy is right. He's absolutely gorgeous. Your husband, sweetie. And now I can't understand why Mason doesn't like him.'

'Where is Kurt?' asked Carlotta, frowning as she looked round the room.

'In the den with Tizzy. He's fixing the stereo.' Ali had hardly finished speaking than a number called Columbia Rock blared out through skilfully hidden speakers. 'It seems he's been successful,' said Ali, clapping her hands in delight. 'Oh, he's just the sort of guy a woman likes to have around the house—practical but, oh, so sexy. Now we can all dance!'

But there was no dancing for Carlotta. She sat with Ethan. It was New Year's Eve all over again, she thought forlornly, as she watched the other couples. No one asked her to dance, but this time it was because everyone thought she wanted to sit with Ethan. And Brad didn't ask her to dance because he preferred to sit out with Tizzy, at the other end of the deck.

At last she couldn't bear sitting there watching others dance any longer. Excusing herself to Ethan, she stood up and went to the other end of the deck.

'It's time we went back to the yacht,' she said curtly to Brad.

'Oh, Carlo, not yet,' Tizzy complained. 'Stay a while longer. Stay the night. We've plenty of room.'

'Thanks for the invitation,' said Brad easily. 'But the skipper is expecting us back on the yacht.'

'Then we'll see you both tomorrow. You said you like playing tennis, Kurt. Come early tomorrow morning and we'll play a few sets.'

'No. We can't come.' Carlotta spoke more sharply than she intended. 'We . . . we're leaving in the morning. Going over to St Kitts and then Nevis,' she added quickly. 'It's been good this evening, Tizzy. Great to see Ethan and your folks.' She slid her hand into the crook of Brad's arm. 'Let's go, darling,' she murmured.

He walked behind her again as they walked down the pathway. Fortunately the moon was up and lit the way. When they reached the jetty Carlotta stopped and swung round to face him and as usual spoke what was in her mind.

'Did you have to stay with Tizzy all evening? Did you have to be so attentive to her?'

He didn't reply immediately. Hands in his pockets in typical casual pose he just stood there looking down at her for a few silent seconds. Then he laughed.

'Don't tell me you're jealous of Tizzy just because I like her, because I repaired the stereo for her and enjoyed talking with her?' he said.

'Jealous? Me? Of Tizzy?' She croaked the words out, trying desperately to cover up with a pretence of scornful surprise her startled reaction to his shrewd observation. 'Why should I be?'

'If you're not, why remark on the fact that I stayed with her nearly all evening?' he taunted. 'What did you expect me to do all evening? Sit around and watch you holding hands with your lame boyfriend while he whispered sweet nothings in your ear?'

'Don't tell me you're jealous of him,' she taunted in her turn, although her voice shook a little.

'Yes, I am. As jealous as hell,' he ground the words out and leaned towards her menacingly. Then he seemed to realise what he had said and withdrew, raking a hand through his hair as he turned away from her. He swore rather virulently and muttered, 'This is damned ridiculous. You have no right to be jealous of Tizzy because I stayed talking to her so that you could spend time with Ethan, and I have no right to be jealous of him because you sat with him.' He laughed rather drearily. 'You know, we're behaving as if we're really married.'

'Or as if . . . as if we've fallen in love with each other,' she whispered.

He turned very slowly and took two long steps back until he was standing right in front of her again. Bending towards her he peered into her face trying to see it by the light of the moon.

'Oh, no,' he murmured. 'I'm not having that. We've only known each other a bare twenty-four hours. I admit we're attracted to each other on a physical level but we're not in love. You're in love with Ethan and he with you!'

'No. I've never been in love with Ethan. I've never been in love with any man,' she said quickly.

'What about Kurt?'

'That . . . that was a foolish infatuation,' she explained, facing up to the truth about her own behaviour with Kurt. 'He . . . he led me on to believe he was something he wasn't. I . . . I realise now I married him only to spite my father. I made a mistake and paid for it.' She paused, then when he remained silent, continued rather breathlessly, 'And now I know I made another mistake in asking you to pretend to be Kurt. They, Tizzy, Ethan and Ali and Caldwell Carter, all had dinner with my father last week. He told them about me having left Kurt and why he disliked him. Now they have met you, they think you're Kurt. They like you and are wondering why my father dislikes you. Oh, Brad. It's such a tangle and I don't know how to undo it.'

'We could go back to the house now—most of

the guests should have left by now—and tell the Carters the truth, if you like, why we got involved in the pretence in the first place,' he suggested quietly. 'Now that I know no harm can come to you from them I'm willing to let them know I'm your bodyguard and why.'

'I suppose you want to see Tizzy again,' she murmured, feeling jealousy raging through her once more. 'You'd want her to know you're not my husband so you can approach her more openly. You like her more than you like me, and . . .'

'No, I don't like her more than I like you,' he said. Raising his hand, he stroked one finger down her cheek in a casual caress and she quivered from head to foot, not in fear, but because the gentle touch of his finger aroused feelings in her she had never experienced before. 'I like you,' he went on softly. 'I like your golden hair, your golden eyes, your golden skin. You're more beautiful than any woman I've ever been close to before. I like you more than I like Tizzy. I like you but I'm not in love with you. I want you but I'm not in love with you. Do you understand what I'm trying to say, Carlotta?'

'No, I don't.' Emotion was boiling up within her and suddenly it burst through the defences she'd been trying to build up for herself. It overflowed. Putting both hands against his chest she lifted her face to his. 'Hold me,' she whispered. 'Hold me closely like you did last night when we were dancing. I felt safe when you held me. I liked being kissed by you too. Please, Brad, hold me, want me because I want you too.'

He groaned as he put his arms around her.

His cheek brushed against hers. She slid her hands up over his shoulders and behind his neck.

'Kiss me,' she said, tipping her head back a little. 'Please kiss me again, like you did last night.'

Gentle at first, his lips parted hers and the night revolved around her, moon and stars spinning. She stroked the nape of his neck and he gasped with pleasure at her touch, the heat of his breath entering her mouth in intimate communion that made her head spin.

They kissed many times, there on the shore with the moon shining down benignly, long sense-shaking kisses that obliterated from Carlotta's mind for ever the distaste she had developed for kissing since her wedding night with Kurt. She found she couldn't have enough of Brad's kisses. Her lips clung to his hungrily and she leaned against him seductively, knowing she was deliberately arousing hem, feeling the power of his leashed-in passion in the way his hands stroked her body through the thin tussore of her tunic.

But at last he raised his head, seemed to tear his lips from hers. Breathing heavily he still held her close to him while he struggled for control. Against her hair, from which he had pulled the pins so that it was now rippling down about her cheeks and over her shoulders, his cheek was hard, pressing through to her head.

After a while he murmured, 'Was that what you wanted, poor little rich girl?' His voice mocked her lightly, belying the passion she could still feel throbbing through him.

'Yes, and more,' she whispered.

He stepped back from her his hands sliding

caressingly down her arms. He lifted both her hands in his, brushed the backs of them with his lips.

'But not now and not here,' he said softly and dropped her hands. 'Lets go back to the yacht before Skip sends a search party to look for us.'

Bemused by his kisses, feeling as if she were walking in a moonlit dream, a dream of a tropical paradise where all her wishes would at last come true, she followed him down to the jetty.

Nothing more was said as the launch zoomed over the flat water, churning up moon-glittered spray. When they reached the yacht Carlotta went up the ladder first and waited on the side-deck for him to join her. Lights glowed softly within the saloon and she wondered if Jilly and Skip were sitting in there.

'I'll tell Skip we've come back,' said Brad crisply turning to her after tying up the launch. 'Shall I tell him also you want to leave here tomorrow morning to go over to St Kitts? Or have you changed your mind and want to go and tell Tizzy and Ethan the truth?'

'I still want to go to St Kitts,' she said. 'Will you be locking me in again, tonight? If so, knock on the cabin door before you do, please.'

'Good night,' he said coolly and walked away from her.

She went down to her cabin. Excitement beat through her as she undressed quickly, put her clothes away and pulled on her nightgown. She removed make-up from her face, brushed her hair, cleaned her teeth.

She had fallen in love again. She knew she had. The knowledge gave her a wonderful feeling of freedom. She was free at last of the anxiety she had felt ever since she realised her mistake in marrying Kurt. She had fallen in love with Brad and she wanted to make love with him. She was normal again, no longer fearing close contact with a man. At least, she didn't fear close contact with Brad, so she must be in love with him. Sitting down on the bunk, she swung her legs up on it, and encircled her knees with her arms to wait for him to knock on the foor. She ached inside with desire.

Some time later she lay down on the bunk. She was trying now to keep her eyes open. She was also trying to ignore a feeling of deep disappointment that was mushrooming inside her, pushing out the earlier joyous feeling of excited anticipation.

She stared at the cabin door willing it to open and for Brad to be there, imagining how he would look at her, his dark eyes lit with the flames of desire. She imagined how she would greet him, inviting him in. Surely he would come soon.

After a while she rolled off the bunk and went over to the door. She would go to look for him, following another wild impulse. She grasped the brass doorknob, turned it and pushed. The door didn't open. It was locked.

Staring at it incredulously, she backed away from it, then, whirling, made for the bathroom. The door in there was locked also. He had come and locked the doors without her hearing him. He had come but he hadn't knocked as she had asked him to. Either he hadn't understood the message she had tried to convey to him, or he had deliberately rejected her invitation.

Shaking off a childish desire to yell and stamp her feet in frustration, Carlotta went slowly back to the bunk and lay down again.

So this was what it was like to love and not be loved in return, to desire and not have that desire satisfied. She switched off the light. It was going to be a very, very, long night.

CHAPTER SEVEN

WHITE paint gleaming, windows glittering with reflected sunlight, the *Montezuma* rolled from side to side on the perpetual surge of the small waves. The yacht was moored in the Bay of Basseterre, an anchorage that was wide open to the sea. On the shore the buildings of the town of Basseterre, capital of the island of St Kitts, white and stone-coloured, seemed to dance in a mirage of heat against the hill slopes behind them, which were bright green with sugar cane. High above the slopes the rugged peak of Mount Misery played hide and seek among purple and grey clouds.

It was almost noon, and Carlotta was on the sun-deck leaning on the rail watching for the return of the yacht's launch with Skipper Atkins. The skipper had gone ashore to report to customs and immigration officials, taking with him the yacht's registration papers and the passports of everyone on board. Once he had cleared with the officials and had received their permission to stay in St Kitts for a few days, passengers and crew would be allowed to go ashore if they wished, or the yacht would cruise to a more comfortable, less rolling anchorage in one of the island's more remote and attractive bays.

Carlotta rested her chin in her hands and her

elbows on the rail. She was wearing cream-coloured bermuda shorts and a sleeveless, multi-coloured shirt. On her head was a wide-brimmed, cream-coloured sun hat, and dark glasses screened her eyes from the bright glare of sunlit water.

She was doing her best to appear at peace with the world and completely happy with her lot. She was lucky, she kept reminding herself, to be there in such a magnificently beautiful place, on such a luxurious yacht with nothing to do except sunbathe or swim. Thousands of young women her age would trade places with her at the drop of a hat, she mused. They would be delighted to give up their jobs in offices, factories or schools or as mothers of tiny tots, just to have one week in the Caribbean sunshine at that time of the year.

But right now she would give everything she possessed just to be one of them, to have a job to go to, to mix with ordinary people, laugh and talk and exchange silly secrets with other women, meet a boyfriend for lunch, go to a movie with him after work and hold hands in the back row of the cinema. Being the daughter of a billionaire, living on a luxury yacht, having nothing to do all day, wasn't all it was cracked up to be if you couldn't go where you wanted when you wanted, or if you couldn't have what you wanted. Being a rich man's daughter was no fun at all when you fell in love with a man who told you to your face that he wasn't in love with you.

She sighed shakily. It was going to be hard meeting Brad again today and behaving as if nothing had happened between them last night. Last night he had kissed her and caressed her as she had always wanted to be kissed and caressed.

Strong yet gentle, he had aroused in her a desire that could be satisfied in only one way and by only one man—*himself*. By every kiss and every caress, he had shown her too that he wasn't a novice when it came to making love to a woman. He had wanted her, she was sure of that.

Then why hadn't he come to her later? Was it because he was already in love with another woman? Did he have a lover in England who was awaiting his return? Or was the woman he loved and to whom he was committed in Nassau?

'Miss Burr, Miss Burr.' Jilly's voice called her from the wheelhouse. 'Your father is on the phone and wants to speak to you. He's calling from St Thomas.'

'St Thomas?' All her daydreams about herself and Brad scattered to the wind as Carlotta ran up the steps to the wheelhouse. 'What's he doing there?'

'I don't know,' said Jilly. 'He wanted to speak to Stan, but when I told him Stan is ashore he asked to speak to you. He came on the VHF radio. You know how to use it, don't you?'

'Of course.'

In the wheelhouse Carlotta picked up the small microphone speaker that was attached to the VHF radio by a telephone wire. She pressed a button on the side of the microphone and spoke into it.

'Carlotta Burr speaking. Hi, Dad. How are you? Over.' She took her thumb off the button so that she would hear him when he spoke. His voice came through very clearly.

'How are you doing, sugar?' Mason Burr's Texan drawl sounded soft and affectionate, a welcome relief to Carlotta after Jilly's and Stan's nasal whines. 'I'm just waiting around here at St Thomas airport while they fill up the plane's tanks with gas so I thought I'd warn you I'll be landing in Morunda about an hour and a half from now. How about grabbing a taxi and going out to the airport to meet me? Over.'

'You're heading for Morunda?' she gasped, realised she hadn't pressed the button and so he couldn't hear her. She pressed it quickly and started all over again. 'Why are you coming to Morunda?'

'Well, that was the arrangement we made, wasn't it, that I'd join you there just as soon as I could get away? This morning when I woke up I said to Cora that today was the day I could get away and she agreed it was time I headed out to see you. Your grandmother, too. She's been mighty worried about you, honey. Mighty worried. We all have. So, are you going to meet me? Over.'

'We . . . the yacht . . . all of us aren't in Morunda right now,' she stammered. 'We're at Basseterre, in St Kitts. Skip Atkins has just gone ashore to clear with customs. Over.'

'Is that so?' His voice drawled more than ever, something that always happened when he was annoyed and Carlotta tensed as she braced herself for an explosion of wrath. 'Well, you can just tell him from me when he returns to the yacht to turn around and go right back to the customs house to get permission to leave. Got that, honey? Over.'

'Yes. But . . .' She paused, realising the futility of arguing with her father. When he issued orders you obeyed him. 'Are you piloting the plane yourself?' she asked, guessing he had flown from Dallas in a series of short hops.

'Sure thing. But Candy is with me.' Candy was the young Mexican he employed to look after the plane and to pilot it when he couldn't. 'Tell Stan I expect the *Monte* to be back in her berth before sunset this evening. I'll be on the dock to catch the lines. It shouldn't take you more than four hours from Basseterre to Morunda. OK? Over.'

'Yes, OK. Take care, Dad. Over and out.'

'You take care, too, sugar. Over and out.'

Carlotta spoke into the microphone again, giving the yacht's call sign and name, said she was returning to the stand-by frequency channel, pressed stand-by numbers on the radio followed by the enter button, then hung up the microphone. Immediately a voice came through calling another yacht in the vicinity. She turned down the volume and turned to Jilly who had returned to the wheelhouse.

'Dad is flying to Morunda. He'll be there in an hour and a half. He wants us to be back at Brock's by sunset today,' she said.

'Oh, bother,' said Jilly mildly. 'Stan won't be at all pleased. He'll have to go straight back to customs to clear us before we can leave.'

'I know. Perhaps we could catch him before he leaves the customs house,' suggested Carlotta. 'We can call them on the VHF, can't we?'

'We can try.' Jilly sounded doubtful. 'We'd have to call the police control and pass the message through them. Anyway, Stan has possibly left customs by now and gone to the market for me.'

'Then our best bet is to send someone ashore

in the other dinghy, to tell him what's happened before he comes back to the boat. How about sending Willy in the Avon dinghy?' suggested Carlotta.

'Willy has already gone ashore with Stan. To visit his family who live in the town.'

'Then I'll go,' said Carlotta. 'It will give me something to do and I'd like to see something of the town, anyway, before we have to leave.'

'Why don't I just ask Brad to go over?' Jilly said. 'If you go, he'll have to go with you anyway.'

'But I want to go,' asserted Carlotta. 'I don't want to have to leave St Kitts without having seen something of it. Go and tell Brad to launch the dinghy and I'll be with him in a few minutes.' She listened to herself giving orders just like her father did with a little flicker of surprise. She had never considered herself autocratic before. 'I just have to pick up my shopping bag and purse from the cabin.'

Before Jilly could present any arguments Carlotta skipped out of the wheelhouse and down the steps to the sun-deck and then to her cabin. Ten minutes later, little sparks of excitement chasing through her at the thought of meeting Brad again, she went up to the main-deck and along to the gate in the rail. The Avon dinghy had been launched and was bobbing on the waves at the ladder, and Brad was standing by the open gate keeping an eye on the dinghy while listening to Jilly who was giving him instructions.

'Good morning, Brad,' said Carlotta, breezily for Jilly's benefit.

'Good morning, miss.' Dark glasses covered

his eyes so it was impossible to see the expression in them. Below the glasses his clean-shaven jaw was taut, his lips unsmiling.

'I was just telling Brad where the only supermarket in the town is located,' Jilly explained. 'If you don't meet Stan returning to the pier you'll find him near the market or on his way back from it. I don't think you'll miss him.'

'I hope we won't,' said Carlotta and made for the gate to go down the ladder. 'I'll drive, Brad,' she said brightly.

Seated in the stern of the little dinghy, she soon had the outboard engine going. Painter in hand, Brad joined her and sat in the bow of the boat, his back to her. The noise of the engine made speech impossible unless they yelled at each other.

From wave to wave the dinghy bounced, sending up showers of glittering spray. Carlotta went at full speed, although she knew from past experience of having sat in the bow of this particular dinghy that the person in the bow would be getting wet. It gave her a certain mischievous pleasure to know that Brad was getting soaked. It was her small revenge on him for having rejected her last night, she thought.

She half-expected him to turn and ask her to go more slowly, or even to move from the bow to the centre thwart. But he didn't turn or move. He just sat there stoically, putting up with the discomfort rather than look at her or speak to her. Stoicism, she guessed, was an important part of his character. Tough, disciplined, stoical. He was all of those, so how could she, naïve and inexperienced as she was, hope to plumb the depths of the passion which she knew now boiled beneath his outer control? How could she rouse him to the point where he would consider the world well lost for the sake of a passionate affair with his employer's daughter?

The pilings of the old pier loomed up, green with slime. Obeying a sign from Brad as he pointed to the left, she steered the dinghy past the end of the pier to the leeward side where there was a floating dock. The yacht's launch was tied up there.

On the pier a row of youths, brown faces shining, white teeth grinning, looked down at Carlotta and Brad as she steered the dinghy to the dock. All of them shouted encouragement to her and two of them leapt down from the pier to the dock. They approached the dinghy, holding out their hands. Both of them were very skinny and were dressed in frayed, cut-off-jeans shorts and ragged T-shirts. Their feet were bare.

'I saw you first, sir. Lemme take your rope and tie it up. Lemme be your guide,' said the bigger of the two.

'I'm Isaac, sir. You won't find no better guide than me in all of St Kitts. Take no notice of him, sir. He's a commie and not to be trusted!'

'Hey, that's not true.' The bigger youth punched at the smaller one who staggered backwards and, realising he was near the edge of the float jumped into the water. The bigger one, losing his balance, also fell into the water. While they were spluttering and laughing, Brad sprang ashore, tied the dinghy painter to one of the pilings of the pier and turned to help Carlotta, holding out a hand to her.

She decided to be independent and with the

handle of her big canvas shopping bag over one
shoulder, sprang ashore just as he had and made
for the broken ladder that led up from the float
to the top of the pier. As she reached the top of
the ladder the rest of the youths, the four who
hadn't jumped down on to the float, crowded
around her, all of them offering to guide her to
the town, buy ice for her, get gas for her if she
paid them a few dollars. Laughingly, she told
them she didn't want a guide, but they still
hopped around her as she walked towards an
open gateway in a steel fence that protected a
long yard behind a warehouse building. Then
suddenly they were all gone, scampering back to
the pier, driven away by sharp authoritative
words from Brad.

Across the yard and into an alleyway between
the warehouse and the next building, high, old-
fashioned and painted a bright turquoise. It was
the customs building and the doors were closed.
A notice stated that the office closed at noon
and re-opened at one o'clock. Carlotta looked at
her watch. The time was ten minutes past twelve.

'He must be at the supermarket or coming
back from there,' she said. 'But as it is he'll
have to wait until one before he can get clearance
for us to leave.' She glanced up at the impassive
face of the man who was standing beside her.
'Did Jilly tell you my father is on his way to
Morunda and expects us to be at the marina by
sunset today?'

'She did.' Cool, indifferent, he didn't look at
her.

'What are we going to do now?' she whispered.

'Find Skip Atkins and be in Morunda by

sunset, I suppose.' He shrugged his shoulders as if the matter didn't concern him.

'I don't mean that and you know I don't. I mean what are you and I going to do about our pretence?'

'Hope that he doesn't find out?' he suggested, shrugging again.

'But if he does?' she persisted.

'Then you'll just have to tell him why you needed an instant husband and hope he'll understand,' he replied coldly.

'Implying that you had nothing to do with it, I suppose,' she retorted, suddenly irritated by his indifference. 'Yet if you hadn't gone along with the idea in the first place and hadn't introduced yourself as Kurt to Bernard, if you hadn't let Tizzy think you were Kurt, there wouldn't have been any pretence.'

'OK.' His voice drawled wearily and he shrugged again. 'Tell him it was my idea if you like. Put the blame on me and he can fire me. I've had enough already of this job of being your bodyguard. It's getting to be boring.'

It was like being stabbed to the heart. She turned to him, only vaguely aware of the noises of the street, the people walking by, cars hooting at each other, the deep shadow on one side, the bright sunlight on the other. His arms folded over his chest, he was standing at ease with his legs apart and he wasn't looking at her.

He was staring back along the street the way they had come, presumably looking for Skipper Atkins.

'That wasn't fair,' she muttered. She couldn't think of anything else to say to express the pain she felt at his wounding remarks.

The dark glasses glinted as he glanced down at her and the rebellious lock of gold-streaked straight dark hair slid forward on to his forehead, but there was no softening of the line of his lips and it seemed to her that his jaw was cast in bronze.

'Love and war seldom are fair,' he retorted coolly. 'Shall we go on now, towards the market? I don't want to miss Skip.'

A hand under her elbow he turned her round and they walked along the narrow street until it widened out into a sort of promenade beside the bay. Palm trees rustled and swayed in the wind blowing off the sea and groups of young men who were walking about shouted to each other. They hadn't gone far when they saw Skip coming towards them, carrying a shopping bag. He was surprised to see them, but grateful when Carlotta explained why they had come.

'Not that I can do much about it now,' he said, as they dawdled back towards the post office. 'I'll have to wait until customs open up again at one. Then they're so slow and meticulous about everything. We'll be lucky if we're able to weigh anchor by two and even luckier if we reach Morunda before sunset.'

'Just as long as we get there today,' said Carlotta consolingly. 'Shall we go and have lunch somewhere while we wait for customs to open? Or is there time for us to take a taxi to Brimstone Hill and visit the fort?'

'I doubt we could get to Brimstone, see the fort and be back here before two,' replied Skip. He lifted his cap and wiped sweat from his forehead on the short sleeve of his shirt. 'Lunch sounds good to me. Wouldn't mind a couple of ice-cold beers. There's a good hotel-restaurant in the Circus. We could sit on the balcony and watch the locals.'

The Circus was so called because it was an oval-shaped space planted with tall palms, with a Victorian-styled clock tower and drinking fountain in the centre. Cars were parked all around the edges of the Circus, and at lunchtime it was full of men, some in smart, tropical, lightweight suits and some in jeans or shorts and T-shirts, eating their lunches from brown paper bags or just lounging about exchanging jokes and gossip. The whole area vibrated with vitality and noise.

'It's a pity we have to go back to Morunda before you've seen much of this island,' said Skipper Atkins. 'It's not a state-of-the-art, tourist-dominated island like Morunda, thank God, although there are excellent hotels where you can stay and fine beaches to swim from.'

'How did it get its name?' asked Carlotta. Brad was silent, almost sullen, she thought, making no effort to join in conversation.

'From Christopher Columbus. He discovered it on his second voyage to the islands,' explained the skipper. 'But the first settlers were English. They established the first British town up the coast at Roadtown. Then the French came and settled here, in Basseterre. British and French lived together fairly amicably until 1666 when all hell broke loose. That was when the British started to fortify Brimstone Hill to protect their settlement. When we leave we'll run up the west coast and you'll see the fort. You could photograph it from the yacht if you have the right lens.'

Carlotta was glad Stan Atkins was a chatterbox

and that his knowledge of the island was intimate, and with the right few words she encouraged him to go on with his potted version of the history of the island.

'When did the French leave?' she asked.

'They said they'd left for ever in 1713,' he returned drily. 'But they were back in the 1780s and forced the British to surrender. They withdrew later and the British regained control. The French returned in 1805 and proceeded to hold this town to ransom. Since then the British had it to themselves until the island received its independence a few years back.' Skip paused, took a deep drink of his second beer and added, 'Talking of ransoms, I take it you've had no trouble keeping an eye on Miss Burr these past few weeks, Brad. No one has tried to grab her?'

'It all depends on what you call trouble,' Brad said slowly, one eyebrow flickering. 'My problem is I never know what she's going to do next!'

Across the table she glared at him, then realised he couldn't see the expression in her eyes because of the sunglasses. If she could have kicked his shin under the table she would have done.

'You must keep him informed, Miss.' Skip Atkins was deadly serious and she experienced a hysterical desire to laugh at the irony of the situation. 'Of where you're going, I mean. And make it possible for him to go with you.'

'I do and I have,' said Carlotta sweetly. 'But I can't help it if Brad allows himself to be distracted by other people when I go visiting. Last night he was far more interested in entertaining my friend Tizzy than he was in protecting me.'

The feline in her knew a certain gloating triumph as she saw Brad's face colour, red running up beneath his tan, and she guessed that if she could have seen the expression in his eyes she would have fallen dead on the spot. She smiled sweetly at him. He scowled and looked away.

Skip Atkins, as if sensing that his two companions were on the verge of war, cleared his throat uncomfortably, finished his beer at a gulp and rose to his feet.

'It's five past one and I'd like to get over to the customs office now,' he said. 'There's just one problem: Willy. He's visiting his mother here in town. I told him to take his time because we wouldn't be leaving until about five to cruise down to Frigate Bay to spend the night there. Someone will have to go and fetch him.'

'Tell me where he is and I'll go and get him,' offered Brad obligingly, also standing up. 'That is, if you think you can keep Miss Burr in order. A visit to customs with you might improve her education. I don't suppose she has much idea of the patience and sheer persistence required to be skipper of a private yacht.'

Suppressing a wilful urge to stick her tongue out at him, Carlotta stood up too.

'I'll be only too pleased to stay with you, Skipper,' she said. 'And to go back in the launch with you. Brad and Willy can return to the yacht in the Avon.'

Outside the hotel, in the noisy, sunny Circus, the skipper gave Brad instructions about where he would find Willy and Brad strode away along a street that went uphill from the Circus. He left her and the skipper as if glad to go, thought

Carlotta as she crossed the Circus with Stan Atkins, glad to be rid of the responsibility of protecting her, if only for a short time.

Yet last night he had told her she was beautiful. Last night he had told her he liked her. Last night he had kissed her as if he had wanted her.

Puzzling over his cold and almost cruel treatment of her that morning and during lunch, she entered the customs building with the skipper. It was a relief to get into the cool, spacious, if shabby, hallway of the old Victorian building and escape from the midday heat. Inside the skipper paused to take off his cap and to wipe sweat from his face and neck while she held his shopping bag. After stuffing his handkerchief into his shorts pocket he gave her a worried glance.

'I'm sorry you're displeased with Brad,' he said rather stiffly. 'But if you're not satisfied with his behaviour you must tell the boss when you see him tonight.' He turned his cap between his hands and stared at it as if it were to blame somehow for his anxiety. 'I didn't think Brad would ever step out of line,' he muttered. 'I suppose I assumed he would do a right good job, be a real professional, when your father asked me for my opinion of him. I recommended him and now I feel responsible for his behaviour . . .'

'But you mustn't feel like that,' Carlotta interposed quickly, cursing herself for her mischievous tongue. 'Brad has done a great job. Really.'

'But you said he paid more attention to your friend last night than to protecting you, and you

know as well as I do, Miss, that a hired
bodyguard isn't supposed to spend his time
socialising with your friends. If you don't tell the
boss I'll have to.'

'No, oh, no. You mustn't do that.' Carlotta's
voice echoed in the high empty hallway. 'I . . . I
was only teasing Brad, at lunchtime. Please don't
you say anything to my father. I'll tell him,
explain everything. It will be all right, I promise
you.'

He didn't look convinced, but he didn't persist,
and, turning away, began to mount a wide
stairway to the next floor. Carlotta followed him,
thoughtfully.

CHAPTER EIGHT

LIKE a luxurious emerald-green tent the island
rose up out of the sea. The lower slopes of the
hills were bathed in golden afternoon sunlight
while white and purple clouds capped the craggy
peaks of its three mountains. From the sun-deck
of the *Montezuma*, which had left the rolling
anchorage of Basseterre at exactly two o clock,
Carlotta surveyed the shore of the island through
the telephoto lens of her camera. Beside her
Skip Atkins did the same. He had left Jilly in
the wheelhouse to supervise the automatic pilot
as the yacht ploughed through the white-crested
waves along the western coast of St Kitts.

Even after they had passed the distinctive and
spectacular Brimstone Hill, an upthrusting mound
of rock surrounded with stone fortifications built
by the British and flat green fields close to the
shore, Carlotta stayed on the sun-deck watching
the rest of the island slide by, forgoing her
afternoon *siesta* and listening to Skip Atkins
talk about the history of the island, about
photography, about anything that came into his
head. He was, it seemed to Carlotta, paying her
a lot of fussy attention, far more than he usually
did and she wondered if—to use a phrase of her
English grandmother—he was buttering her up
for some reason.

When the yacht reached the north-west point of St Kitts the skipper left her to return to the wheelhouse to supervise a change of course and Jilly came down to join Carlotta, to chatter cheerfully of this and that, increasing Carlotta's suspicion that the skipper and his wife were worried about what she was going to say to her father when she met him in Morunda.

The bow of the yacht turned to the right, to starboard, and they entered the wide channel between the north end of St Kitts and the Dutch island of St Eustatius, called locally Statia. Its volcanic peak half-hidden under a puffy white cloud, the small island looked like a flattened Dutchman's cap made from green and yellow felt.

Called back to the wheelhouse by the skipper, Jilly left the sun-deck and, alone, Carlotta saw the hills of Morunda appear on the horizon as the yacht surged out of the channel and into the open sea again. The weather was changing. As often happened between three and five in the afternoon the trade wind was increasing in strength. Fast-moving clouds frolicked across the sea from the south-east. The water was darkened by their shadows and churned up by the strengthening wind.

Slanting rain hit the yacht. Carlotta ran for shelter into the saloon. The yacht rolled and lurched under the onslaught of the sudden squall. Jilly appeared through the other entrance to the saloon.

'Are you all right, miss?'

'Sure I am,' said Carlotta. 'Do you know where Brad might be?'

'In his cabin. He said he was going to catch

up on his sleep this afternoon since there was nothing much for him to do?' Jilly gave her a curious yet wary glance. 'Skip has been telling me you're not too happy with Brad's behaviour....'

'Oh, no, no. I told Skip not to worry about what I said to Brad.' Her suspicions had been right then. Skip and Jilly were worried about what she might say to her father, not so much about them but about Brad. 'I was only teasing Brad at lunchtime. I'm not going to complain about him to Dad,' she added, irritated with herself because she been so outspoken in front of Skip Atkins.

'You might tell him that, then.' Jilly was still looking anxious.

'I will. Which is his cabin?'

'Number four in the fo'c'sle,' Jilly replied without hesitation, her face resuming its usual expression of cheeriness. 'But I expect he'll be up on deck before we reach Morunda. You could say something to him then, just to relieve his mind, I think he believes you're going to have him sacked, miss.'

'All right. I'll see him, then. I'll just go and put my camera away now. The squall seems to have passed through.'

But although the rain had stopped, the clouds had rolled on and the sun was shining again, the yacht was still lurching about on the bigger waves and Carlotta had to hang on to the rail of the companionway as she made her way down to the lower deck. In her cabin, she stowed her camera carefully in the bag where she kept all her photographic equipmentand put the bag in the locker. She had learned the hard way when she had first cruised on the yacht not to leave

anything valuable or breakable lying about
carelessly. In a sudden squall like the one they
had just had anything could go flying across a
cabin and break if it hadn't been chocked off
and prevented from sliding about a shelf.

Her camera put away, she lay down on the
bunk thinking she, like Brad, might also catch
up on her sleep. What a nuisance she must seem
to Skip and Jilly, she thought, with her impulsive
behaviour and her way of speaking without
thinking. She had never considered before how
responsible they might feel for her well-being.
Nor had she ever thought how dependent they
were on her good opinion of them. Their jobs,
she realised with another flicker of irritation at
herself, depended on her giving a good report of
them to her father.

How would her father react when he learned
of her latest escapade? She would have to tell
him that she had asked Brad to pretend to be
her husband before he ran into Phillida or
Bernard. He might be angry with her but he
would be more so with Brad. He might sack
Brad on the spot and then sack Skip and Jilly
for having recommended Brad.

As for Brad, what was he thinking now about
her? Cold and sardonic this morning, he had
said he had found being her bodyguard boring.
With a few calculated and cruel remarks he had
set her at a distance, and now he must be
thinking that his own opinion of her was right.
She was a person who never thought.

An urge to go and find him and to explain she
had been only teasing him about Tizzy at
lunchtime was very strong. She didn't want to
wait until he was on deck and preparing for the

docking of the yacht at the marina on Morunda.
She wanted to talk to him now, to cross the
distance he had made between himself and her,
to get close to him again.

Yet the urge bothered her. Was it just another
wild whim, an impulse she would regret later?

Slowly she rolled off the bunk and went over
to the door. She opened it and looked out into
the passageway. Save for the humming of the
engines and the swishing of the sea against the
hull, all was quiet. Slowly, she stepped over the
high sill and closed the cabin door. For just a
moment she hesitated, before making her way
forward along the central passage to the door
that separated the crew's quarters in the fo'c'sle
from the owner's and guest cabins in the after
part of the yacht.

Cabin number four was the first she came to
after stepping into the fo'c'sle. Again she
hesitated before knocking on the door, her
cheeks flushing red at her own effrontery in
actually coming this far. Never before in her life
had she pursued a man. Always she had been
the pursued not the pursuer. And never had she
intruded on anyone's privacy before. She prized
her own privacy too much ever to have done
that.

But the urge to see Brad and to talk to him
was fast developing into a raging torrent that
was sweeping all puritan reserve before it. She
raised her fist and knocked sharply on the door.

Nothing happened, and in a down-swirl of
anticlimax she turned the doorknob and pulled
the door open, fully expecting to see an empty
cabin and drawing a sharp breath of surprise
when she saw Brad lying on the bottom one of

two bunks, his back to the door. He was dressed only in the white uniform shorts and the skin of his long wide back shone, smooth as reddish-brown silk, tempting her hands.

The cabin was much smaller than hers, only about six feet wide, and when she stepped in and closed the door after her she found she was standing very close to him, close enough to be tempted even more to slide her fingers over his shoulders, to ruffle his already tousled hair, to bend close to him and whisper in his ear.

Instead, hands clenched at her side, she stood still and upright, her feet apart as she adjusted her balance to the lift and roll of the yacht and said loudly, 'Brad. Wake up. I must talk to you.'

Muscle rippled beneath smooth skin as he stiffened. For a moment he lay still yet alert. Then he moved, turning and sitting up all in one movement, raking back his hair. She saw his face harden and his eyes narrow to slits.

'What the hell are you doing in here?' he demanded. 'Get out.'

As she had guessed, he was angry with her for having intruded and, hurt by his reaction, she almost turned and fled. But the magnetism between them had begun its subtle action. It seemed to glue her feet to the spot, her gaze to his upturned face.

'I knocked but you didn't answer,' she explained haltingly. 'I . . . I only opened the door to look in to see if you were here . . .'

'I was dozing,' he cut in coldly. 'You didn't have to come in. Looking in would have been enough. Now, go away.'

'But I must talk to you,' she argued.

'Then give me a couple of minutes to put on a shirt and I'll come up to the saloon,' he replied crisply. 'Go on, get out. There's hardly room for me in this cabin, never mind you as well. I can't put on a shirt with you in here.'

'You don't have to put on a shirt,' she said. The boat gave a bigger lurch than usual and she lost her balance and, turning quickly, sat down on the edge of the bunk beside him. 'I can say what I have to say here. No one will interrupt us or overhear us.'

'I would rather hear what you have to say in the saloon.' He inched away from her along the bunk, his expression hostile. Suddenly he swore, a crisp crashing oath uttered between taut lips and she flinched. 'Why did you have to come in here?' he demanded in a goaded voice. 'The one place where I can escape from you?'

That hurt more than anything else he had said to her. She stiffened, hiding her hurt as always beneath a pose of hauteur.

'It won't take long. I just wanted you to know I'm sorry about what I said at lunch,' she said in flat, controlled voice, not looking at him but at the opposite wall of the cabin covered with built-in lockers. 'About you and Tizzy. I only said it to get back at you for some of the nasty remarks you'd made to me,' she continued. 'And I realise now that it upset Skip Atkins. He and Jilly think I'm going to complain to my father about you and about them for recommending you. But it's all right. I won't be complaining about you or them and I won't be blaming you for the pretence. I know you wouldn't have pretended to be Kurt

if I hadn't asked you. I know I'm to blame for
what happened.'

She paused. He didn't speak. The silence
was laden with tension and the atmosphere in
the small cabin was stifling. Outside the few
inches of thick fibreglass and insulation that
separated them from the sea, water swished
and sprayed against the hull as the yacht surged
forward.

'But I'll have to tell Dad about it. I'll have
to tell him before Phillida or Bernard or anyone
else tells him they know Kurt is with me,'
Carlotta muttered, looking down at her hands
which were gripping each other nervously on
her knee. 'You do see that, don't you?'

'Yes, I see it.' He spoke coldly. 'But I've
already told you I don't care if he does decide
to give me the sack.'

'Oh, but I do.' She turned to him, her
control swamped by a flood of emotion.

'Well, well, this is quite a change from
yesterday morning,' he jeered. 'Yesterday you
were all set to phone him to ask him to fire
me. Carlo, Carlo, quite contrary!'

'Oh, stop it, stop it!' She clapped her hands
over her ears. 'Stop making fun of me.'

The mockery faded from his face. It became
as blank and hard as a statue's.

'Then get out of here,' he said clearly and
loudly so that she could hear him through her
hands.

'Not yet.' She dropped her hands on to her
lap again. Pride dictated that she should leave
when he had made it so clear he didn't want
her in his cabin, but she still had something to
say. 'I know I must seem contrary,' she said,

not looking at his face but at his powerful thigh, so close to hers. If she reached out one hand she could touch it, stroke the bare skin, feel the muscle and sinews tauten beneath her fingers. The need to touch him, to let magnetism have its way, was causing her to ache inside. Her hands clenched again and she looked away, down at the floor of oak strips. 'But, then, so much has happened since yesterday morning,' she added with a sigh.

'Has it? I hadn't noticed.' Abrupt, acidic, his remark seared her, but she refused to be deterred by his jeers. Swallowing hard, sinking her pride, she raised her head and looked directly at him. He looked back at her, his dark eyes wary as he leaned away from her, resting his back against the wall at the head of the bunk.

'I waited for you last night,' she said as steadily as she could. 'I hoped that when you came to lock the doors of my cabin you would knock first. Why didn't you?'

'I decided that discretion was the better part of valour,' he replied coolly.

'So what's that supposed to mean?' she demanded sharply. Was there no way she could get through his steely defences? 'Don't talk to me in riddles. Give it to me straight in basic English.'

His eyes widened a little, but his expression was still hard.

'All right, you asked for it,' he said harshly. 'This is as straight and as basic as I can get. I decided not to betray Mason J. Burr's trust in me by laying his daughter.'

Carlotta flinched. She couldn't help it even

though she guessed he was deliberately trying to antagonise her by reducing what might have happened in her cabin the previous night to its lowest and, for her, most insulting terms.

'That was insulting.' she whispered.

'It was meant to be. Your father hired me to protect you, not to sleep with you. You've said what you came here to say, so get out of here. Go.' Hard and cold as bullets his words hit her but she didn't move.

'Why? Why are you trying to hurt me?' she asked shakily. 'Last night you told me you like me and you kissed me and touched me as if you wanted me. It seems to me your feelings are as contrary as mine, blowing hot then cold.' She leaned towards him suddenly, trapping him. He drew a sharp breath and closed his eyes. 'Brad, be honest with me,' she pleaded. 'Was the thought that you'd be betraying my father's trust in you the only reason why you didn't come to me last night?'

Muscles ridged along his jaw. His eyelids quivered but he didn't open his eyes.

'Yes,' he admitted slowly between taut lips. 'It was the only reason. Now, go.'

'No.'

His eyes flashed open. She was so close to him now she could see that the little flecks in the dark brown irises appeared red by contrast and as he stared into her eyes it seemed to her that those flecks widened until his eyes glowed fierily.

'You don't know what you're doing,' he whispered, lips still taut. 'When Mason J. Burr hired me he didn't say anything about having to protect you from yourself, from your own wild impulses, nor did he say I would have to fight like hell to keep you at a distance. He didn't tell me that you're a dangerous and fascinating woman, an irresistible temptress. For your own sake, Carlotta, more than mine, will you get to hell out of here?'

Sweat glistened on his shoulders and on the warm brown column of his neck. Giving in to temptation that was also wrecking her last few restraints, Carlotta put a hand on his right shoulder, sliding it over his moist skin. His teeth snapped together as he snarled at her, his lips only a few inches from hers.

'Get out. Go away. Leave me alone.'

She bent her head, the silken wiriness of her hair brushing his face and put her lips to the pulsing hollow at the base of his throat. His skin was salt-tasting. Desire zig-zagged through her, seeming to rip apart all control. Lifting her head a little, she looked up at him through his lashes.

'I can't go now,' she murmured. 'I've fallen in love with you and I want you. You don't really want me to go away and leave you alone now, do you?'

He swore at her, but she could tell he wasn't intending to insult her. He was swearing at himself more than at her.

'Have you any idea what you do to a man when you look at him like that?' he groaned. 'You did it last night on the deck at the Carters' place and I had trouble keeping my hands off you then.'

'You haven't answered my question. Do you really want me to go?' she said, lowering her eyelids, trying not to influence him with a look.

'No, I don't want you to go,' he admitted reluctantly. 'But I think you should.'

'You ought to know by now that I never do what I should do and I always do what I like to do,' she teased him lightly. 'Also, I wouldn't like you to be too bored while you're my bodyguard,' she added.

'For God's sake . . .' he began hoarsely and didn't finish what he was going to say because his lips swooped to hers, swift as an eagle swoops to its prey.

This time he showed no restraint. His tongue thrust into the sweet, moist hollow of her mouth and his fingers closed roughly about her breasts. A series of exquisite sensations corkscrewed through her, right down to the pit of her stomach. Dizzy with desire and heady triumph because she had at last got beneath his guard, she pressed against him eagerly. Her hands twined in his hair to hold his head still so that he couldn't avoid her response to his kiss. Deftly, his hands at her waist, he shifted himself and her until they were lying facing each other on the narrow bunk, their mouths clinging, their breasts touching, their legs entwining.

The yacht plunged on, through and over waves. Water still swished along the smooth hull and gurgled in the forward scuppers. Up and down the bunk tilted, rolling a little from side to side, but lying close to Brad Carlotta heard nothing of the sound of water, felt nothing of the pitch and roll.

Swept by passion as sudden and intense as a tropical squall into a purely sensual word of chaotic nerve-tingling caresses, her mind drugged with the scent of human hair and sunkissed skin, her ears deafened by her own heartbeats, she knew nothing of her surroundings and cared less. A hunger to possess and be possessed was consuming her, a ravenous pagan desire that was swelling and swelling with every touch of Brad's devastating fingers, with every nip of his teeth, with every scorching pressure of his lips against hers.

At first they didn't speak. They were too breathless. And words weren't needed. Touch was enough. Skin to skin they shifted against each other until they were both on fire with delight and aching to be closer. When Brad did speak she heard his voice, thick with passion, faintly through the drumming in her ears.

'Don't be afraid, love. I won't hurt you, but there's no going back now.'

Wondering vaguely how he knew that, for a while, she had dreaded that act on the edge of which they were both teetering, Carlotta managed to whisper, 'I don't want to back out. I love you and want you.'

And then suddenly it was over, the part she had feared most, and she was closer to Brad than she had ever been. They seemed to be dancing again, moving in unison, and all the chaotic sensations were fusing together. Her head was filled with coloured lights whirling in the darkness like a strobe light in a discothèque.

The beat of erotic music drummed in her ears, sensations swam together and swelled in a huge wave that lifted her up and up. Everything stopped, the music, her heart, the revolving coloured lights. Weightless, thoughtless, she floated through space as gentle as a feather before drifting down to the swish of water against the hull close beside her, the slight roll and shudder of the yacht and the weight of Brad's head on her shoulder, the feel and taste of his hair in her mouth, the slackness of his body lying half on and half off her.

Then it came, the feeling of sweet secret satisfaction because she had got what she had wanted.

A sudden sharp rap of knuckles on the door of the cabin made Brad stiffen and roll away from her. Standing up he snatched up clothing from the floor, tossed her shirt and shorts on to her without looking at her and turned away to pull on his own shorts.

'Who it it?' he yelled and moved to the door, putting a hand on the knob to hold it shut if anyone should try to open it.

'Me, man,' Willy's deep voice with its lilting Caribbean accent answered. 'We're just pulling into Morrisburg Bay. Skip says to get the line ready for docking. Hey, man, be looking lively.'

'OK, I'll be with you in a couple of seconds.'

Still half stunned by the completeness of her capitulation to his love-making, Carlotta lay on the bunk, her shirt and shorts lying across her breasts and legs. Through her down-drooping lashes she watched Brad pull on his T-shirt, secretly admiring the play of muscle beneath his skin. For a few moments of passion he had been hers, entirely hers. She hugged the knowledge to herself. No matter what happened now, no matter what cruel jibes he made, she would remember his loving tenderness during those few moments for ever.

He thrust his feet into his sneakers and bent

to lace them up. On his way to the door he paused and turned to slant an enquiring glance at her.

'Are you all right?' he asked, and his obviously sincere concern for her well-being touched her heart.

'I'm fine,' she replied smiling at him. 'And you?'

'What do you think?' He parried her question with one of his own as if he didn't want to admit how good he felt.

He turned to the door and grasped hold of the knob then looked back at her again.

'But don't ever try it on with me, again,' he cautioned coldly. 'That clear?'

'Oh, why not?' In the face of his harshness all the lovely warm feeling of fulfilment was fading rapidly.

'Because you and I can't . . .' he started and broke off with a muttered curse, turning his head away from her. 'Oh, hell, because oil and water don't ever mix, I guess,' he added roughly, pushed open the door and stepped into the passage. The door closed with a slam.

Thoroughly confused, Carlotta swung off the bunk and staggered as the yacht changed course sharply, swinging to starboard again. Through the porthole she could see the surface of the sea, red as blood reflecting the sunset. The yacht rolled and she saw a dark headland at the end of which a light was flashing.

While she and Brad had been drowned in passion the sun had dropped below the horizon and the yacht had reached Morunda. Her father had got his way as he usually did. The *Montezuma* would be in its berth at Brock's marina just after six, a few minutes only after the sun had set.

She pulled on her shorts and shirt, thinking of Brad and the final riddle he had flung at her. Oil and water don't mix. Well, she knew that. But who was the oil and who the water? Herself and him, no doubt. And why shouldn't they mix? Hadn't they just proved to each other that they could be fused together in the excitement and pleasure of making love?

But perhaps it hadn't been as pleasurable for him as it had been for her, she thought disconsolately as she left his cabin. After all, she was only a beginner. She wasn't as experienced as he was, and didn't know yet what would give him most pleasure. She could learn, though. She was eager to learn from him, but only from him, and how could she learn from him or about him if they didn't do it again?

Don't try it on with me again. Nasty, sneering words designed to make her hate him.

Why? Oh, forget the bit about oil and water. Forget, too, his excuse about not wanting to betray her father's trust in him. There had to be another reason for his resistance. He didn't love her. Well, she could accept that. She knew men weren't like women. She knew a man didn't have to be in love to make love. She loved him enough to overcome that.

He was probably in love with someone else, a woman in London or even Nassau. A woman to whom he wasn't married, it was true, but with whom he had established a permanent relationship and with whom he was emotionally involved.

As she opened the door of her own cabin and stepped inside it seemed as if her spirits sank to an all-time low. From the dizzy heights of ecstasy to the dark depths of despair in less than fifteen minutes. She sank down on her bunk and stared before her, seeing nothing of the cabin, seeing only the future, her own future, hours, days, months and years of loving Brad while he loved another woman.

CHAPTER NINE

THE bumping of the yacht against the dock, the squeaking sound of fenders as they took the load and the subsequent stopping of the engines all penetrated Carlotta's consciousness and roused her from the cold lethargy into which she had sunk. With a sigh she stood up and went through to the bathroom. She undressed and stepped into the shower stall. She stood under the sluicing hot water for a long time, finding a certain confort in its heat. When she had done she wrapped a towel around herself and returned to the main cabin, found her hair-dryer and plugged it in, thankful that along with all its other luxuries the yacht had two hundred and twenty volt electricity for the running of cookers, refrigerators, water heaters—and her simple hair-dryer.

When her hair was dry she dressed again, this time in narrow white trousers and a loose, navy blue top splattered with white, crimson and blue flowers. Around her hair she wound a long silk scarf, also crimson-coloured, wearing it low on her forehead, and she was just making up her face when someone knocked on the door. Her heart leapt and her cheeks flamed. Could it be Brad, returning from having helped tie the yacht to the dock and stopping on his way to his cabin to explain his riddle and about oil and water?

Knuckles rapped again. A voice called to her. Jilly's voice. Her heart slowed, the colour faded from her cheeks.

'Come in,' she called out and continued to apply lipstick as she held a mirror before her and watched her lips take on the colour of poppies.

'Mr Burr is on board now, miss,' Jilly announced from the open doorway. 'He's in the saloon and would like you to join him and his guests for drinks.'

'Guests?' Carlotta looked up sharply. 'He has guests?'

'Yes. Mr and Mrs Chalmers and Mr and Mrs Digby. Shall I tell Mr Burr you're on your way, miss?'

'Yes—er, yes, please. Tell him . . .' She broke off as a sudden swift thought shot into her mind. 'No, would you mind asking my father, Jilly, if he would come down here? Say there's something I must tell him that's very important and that I can't discuss in front of his guests. Try and make it sound really urgent, Jilly. Because it is.'

'All right, miss. I'll do my best, miss.'

'Thanks.' Carlotta smiled her best and most charming smile. 'You're a dear, Jilly, and you needn't worry. I won't be complaining to him about you, or Skip or about Brad. But I must speak to him in private.'

'Yes, miss.' The anxious lines around Jilly's eyes changed into crinkles of good humour as she smiled back. 'And thank you, miss. Skip and I appreciate what you've just said, miss, and I'd just like to add it's been a pleasure having you on board these past few weeks.'

Jilly went out and closed the door. Flinging

aside the make-up mirror and tube of lipstick, Carlotta sprang to her feet and began to pace about the small cabin nervously. What she had hoped to avoid had happened. Her father had met Phillida before she had been able to explain to him about Brad pretending to be Kurt, and she knew Phillida well enough to realise that the woman would have no hesitation in telling Mason Burr she had at last met his son-in-law.

What had been her father's reaction to Phillida's announcement? She was surprised he hadn't come storming down to her already to demand what the hell was going on. But perhaps that was why he had sent Jilly to ask her to go up to the saloon. Perhaps he had intended to confront her about the reappearance of Kurt in front of Phillida, Gordon and the Digbys, to surprise and embarrass her into stuttering out the truth in from of them.

She stopped pacing to linger by the porthole. The lights from the marina building twinkled in the dark blue tropical night. She could hear the familiar beat of of Columbia Rock. There would be no band at the marina tonight, but the bartenders would be playing their favourite numbers on the cassette player. The sound of the music brought back memories of New Year's Eve, of herself and Brad sitting on the patio at separate tables, occasionally glancing at each other.

Pressing her fists against her temples, she swung around and began pacing again. Oh, God, why had she asked him to dance with her? Why had she given in to that crazy impulse to ask him to pretend to be her husband? And above all, why had he gone along with the idea? Had he been moon-mad too? Had some strange erotic impulse stirred in him? Lonely like her, had he jumped at the chance to dance with someone, to be with someone to celebrate the New Year?

She had only herself to blame for the tangle she was in. She mustn't blame him at all. She had made all the initial moves, even this afternoon. *Don't try it on with me again.* Oh! she gasped painfully as if she had been punched, and sat down on the bunk. Why did he hurt her so? Why was he always rejecting her?

Fingers tapped a tattoo on her door, the knob turned, the door opened and her father looked in. Slim and straight in a well-tailored white tuxedo, his shirt crisply ruffled, his bow tie perfectly arranged and his brushed-back, silvery hair shining under the electric light, he stepped over the sill and closed the door. Leaning against it he looked at her with shrewd grey eyes.

'I believe you have something very important to tell me in private,' he said and his Texan drawl was soft and affectionate.

'Oh, Dad. It's good to see you.' Across the room Carlotta flung herself, her arms going out to him. He caught her against him and kissed her cheek. Tears spurted from her eyes and she hid her face in his shoulder.

'Now, now, sugar. What's all this?' he asked, pushing her gently from him so he could see her face. 'Tears. From you? I thought you despised women who weep.'

'Not any more. I've found out there are times when you have to weep,' she said, sniffing and flicking away the tears from her cheeks with a finger. 'And this is one of them. I . . . thought after that row we had in Vienna you and I would never be friends again, that you would never forgive me for going against your wishes and marrying Kurt.'

'Ah, yes. Kurt,' he murmured. 'He's here, so Phillida tells me. Arrived New Year's Eve.' His grey glance, bright and observant, swept round the cabin. 'I don't see him in here or any signs of his occupancy.' His glance came back to her, his grey eyes hard, brilliant as diamonds. 'Am I to assume he survived the hunting accident and didn't break his neck after all? And are you and he reconciled?'

'Oh, please, Dad, don't go all upstage and haughty on me,' she pleaded. 'Sit down and I'll explain.' He sat down on the settee berth and she sat again on the bunk. 'I hoped to see you before Phillida did, to explain. Kurt was killed, as I told you in my letter. It was an awful shock to me, the news, but I'm over it now and I realise his death solved a lot of problems for me.'

'Then if he's dead, how come Phillida met him on New Year's Eve?' Mason interrupted her.

'I . . . I asked Brad to pretend to be my husband,' she said quickly. 'It . . . it was all I could think of to keep Bernard off my back.'

'Now let's get this straight.' Mason Burr held up a hand and tapped the index finger with the index finger of the other hand. 'First, Brad. I guess you mean Tristan Bradley, the guy I hired to be your bodyguard? Second, Bernard. Would that be Bernard Digby?'

'Right. Dad, Bernie was most . . . well, most obnoxious, pestering me all the time, and to put him off I told him Kurt would be joining me on the yacht on New Year's Eve. So when Bernie turned up here at the marina on New Year's Eve, I asked Brad to dance with me and to pretend to be Kurt if Bernie made himself objectionable.'

'And I guess Bernie made himself objectionable,' drawled Mason. 'So Brad became Kurt.'

'And then Phillida came up to us and we . . . I had to go on with the pretence because Bernie was still there.'

'I see. You mischievous little devil!' he murmured and began to laugh.

'There's more, Dad,' she warned and his face sobered.

'More. OK, tell me the worst,' he said with a sigh of resignation and she told him why Brad had ordered the skipper to leave Morunda to save her the embarrassment of having to explain to Bernard and Phillida that they had been tricked on New Year's Eve, and how they had decided to continue with the pretence when they had gone to the Carters' party.

'Although Tizzy really brought that on herself,' Carlotta complained. 'When she saw Brad she just assumed he was Kurt, fell over herself trying to impress him. It was quite sickening.'

'You like him?' Mason Burr asked abruptly and, realising that she had said more than she had intended, had perhaps given herself away to this shrewd man who was her father, she gave him a quick glance. He was looking at her narrowly.

'Like whom?' she asked, pretending to be surprised.

'Brad. Tristan Bradley.'

'He's . . . he's done his job very professionally,'

she said coolly, but was unable to control the
rush of blood to her cheeks. Nor could she look
him in the eyes.

'Hmm. Sounds to me as if he's been a tab too
professional, pretending to be your husband,'
drawled Mason menacingly.

'Oh, you're not to blame him for it!' Carlotta
rose to the bait too quickly, giving herself away
again, although she didn't realise it. 'It was all
my fault. I'm to blame for the mess I'm in now.
Dad, what am I going to do about Phillida?
When she mentioned that Kurt was with me,
what did you say? Did you tell her he was
dead?'

'I said nothing,' he replied. 'I have to admit I
was a bit shaken but I hope I'm a good enough
actor not to have shown it. I let her ramble on
and held my peace, thinking I'd find out just
exactly what was going on from you first.' He
rose to his feet. 'They've gone, Phillida and
Gordon and the Digbys, but I said we'd join
them for dinner at Jonathan's.' Jonathan's was
an all-American restaurant situated on the hill
behind the marina. 'You ready to go now?'

'But what am I going to say to Phillida about
Brad not being Kurt?'

'Brad doesn't have to come to dinner too,' he
said.

'But have you forgotten? He's my bodyguard.
He goes everywhere I go.'

'He doesn't have to go where you go tonight,'
he drawled, turning to the door. His hand on
the knob he turned to her. 'Don't worry about
it, honey. All you have to say is that Kurt has
gone back to Europe. You can even dress it up
a bit and say you and he have had a tiff and you

hope you'll never see him again. Then later in the year, much later we can let it out to friends and family that he's dead. It's just a case of postponing his death.'

'But . . . but supposing Philllida or Bernie sees Brad, here at the marina? Bernie often comes down to the bar here and we can't ask Brad to stay aboard ship all the time,' she exclaimed.

'Leave it to me,' he said firmly. 'I'll have a word with Brad right now, tell him he doesn't have to come with us tonight because I'll be with you. You just remember what you're going to say to Phillida and the others when they ask where Kurt is. It will work out OK, honey. I promise you. Now where will I find Brad?'

'Probably in his cabin. Number four in the fo'c'sle,' she said dully. Then, on a sudden thought she sprang to her feet. 'But you won't sack him, will you, Dad? Please.'

'Just leave it to me, sugar,' he said soothingly. 'Everything will be all right. I'll join you in a few minutes in the saloon before going ashore.'

He was much longer than a few minutes, and she had been waiting in the saloon nearly half an hour, pacing up and down nervously, wondering what was being said below decks, fearful that her father might do the very thing she had tried to avoid and would sack Brad. Several times she thought of going down to Brad's cabin to interfere, but every time she controlled the impulse. Hard experience had taught her to be careful where her father was concerned. If she showed too much interest in Brad he would guess she had fallen in love with her bodyguard and he would do everything in his power to stop the affair.

When Mason eventually appeared she tried to appear unconcerned, although she observed his face closely for any signs of anger. But he was too good a poker player to betray any signs of emotion, and in the end she had to ask, as they left the yacht and walked along the dock, if everything was all right.

'Sure it's all right. We had a good laugh over your little charade. I explained to him what we were going to do about it tonight and he agreed that it was a good idea. So that's that.'

'But . . . supposing Phillida and Bernie see Brad while the yacht is still here?'

'They won't. You see, sugar, that's why I flew down today. We're leaving Morunda in the morning and going over to the Virgin Islands. Cora and Granny Liz are flying to St Thomas today and will join us there. Then we'll go over to the island of Culobra to visit the Erlandsons and from there cruise the south coast of Puerto Rico before making for the Bahamas. I'd like Atkins to take the yacht back to Texas for the spring. It needs some attention. You'll come on the cruise with us, of course.'

'I suppose so,' she murmured.

Jonathan's turned out to be a good choice of place in which to meet Phillida, Gordon and the Digbys, Carlotta thought later, when she sat at a table in a long room with a cathedral ceiling that looked out from the hillside over the light-twinkling harbour to the dark shapes of hills on the other shore. It was full of American tourists, and the noise of their loud voices filled the room. To make oneself heard by one's neighbour one had to shout.

Phillida seemed to lose interest in the subject

of Kurt when Carlotta told her that he had returned to Europe, and it wasn't necessary to say anything about having quarrelled with him. Since there were some acquaintances from New York at the table also, Phillida was much more interested in them. Bernard, Carlotta learned from his parents, had returned to the States. Soon it seemed to her that she had worried about nothing, and when she lay on her bunk later that night, sleepless, the panic she had experienced at seeing Bernard on New Year's Eve, which had driven her into asking Brad to dance with her and to masquerade as her husband, seemed now to have been part of a dream.

But had she asked Brad to dance with her only because she had seen a way to avoid Bernard? With a groan she faced up to the reality of her feelings about Brad. Why not admit that she had been attracted to him from the first time she had seem him when she had come aboard the yacht at the beginning of December? For a month she had watched him covertly, had felt a certain thrill of excitement whenever she had noticed him in a street or disco, and had wondered then if he had been following her because he had been attracted to her too.

Now she knew he had been following her for an entirely different reason. He had followed her to protect her. There was something very romantic about having a bodyguard like him, she thought dreamily, and wished he would be around to protect her for ever from men like Bernard, or even Kurt. She wished Brad could be her *real* husband. But that was something that seemed beyond her reach now.

She slept little as she tussled with this new problem, slipping into slumber only towards dawn. She woke later to the sound of the yacht's engines. Hurrying, she showered and dressed and went up to the saloon. The yacht was well out to sea and the hills of Morunda were sinking fast below the line of the eastern horizon. Ahead the sea stretched glittering with sunlight, green, turquoise and purple, moving perpetually under the arching cloudless blue sky.

'Mr Burr and Skip have already had breakfast,' Jilly announced as she came into the saloon. 'I'm sorry I didn't have time to wake you earlier with some juice, miss. I had to help with the dock lines.'

'Why was that? I thought Brad always helped Willy with the lines,' said Carlotta.

'Brad isn't with us any more. He left yesterday evening for Antigua, soon after you'd gone ashore,' replied Jilly.

Shock made Carlotta sit down suddenly on one of the chairs. She watched Jilly pour coffee for her.

'Do you know why he left?' she asked when she could speak.

'He just said the time had come for him to leave.'

'He wasn't sacked, was he, Jilly?' Carlotta asked hoarsely.

'Not as far as I know. He and your dad parted on good terms, I believe. I gather you didn't complain to Mr Burr about Brad's behaviour.'

'No, I didn't.' She discovered she was feeling cold. The coffee she had gulped down was tasteless and no help at all. Jilly, do you know where he's gone?' she whispered.

Jilly glanced at her, a slight frown pleating her brow.

'Are you all right, miss? You're looking a bit pale. Don't feel sick, do you? They say there's been a lot of food poisoning on the island. Some of those restaurants aren't too hygienic and the kitchen staff aren't as particular as they could be about the preparation of food and so much of the meat is frozen and then not cooked thoroughly.'

'No. I'm not sick, Jilly. But I don't think I'll have anything to eat. I suppose my father is in the wheelhouse?'

'That's right, miss. He says we're going to pick up Mrs Burr and your grandmother in St Thomas. I'm really looking forward to meeting the old lady again.'

'So am I,' said Carlotta, brightening up a little and sliding off the berth. 'I'll go and join Dad,' she murmured.

Her heart felt like a lump of lead in her chest as she mounted the steps to the wheelhouse. Or was it just the cold coffee lying unswallowed somewhere in her gullet, she wondered with a wry grin at herself? She slid open the door to the wheelhouse and entered its air-conditioned coolness. Her father was alone, looking through his binoculars at a freighter that was coming towards the yacht, and the automatic pilot was steering. From the VHF came the sound of a voice calling the harbour master at Morrisburg from another yacht.

'Did you fire Brad last night?' Carlotta attacked right away.

Mason lowered the binoculars and turned to smile at her. He leaned towards her and kissed her on one cheeks.

'Morning, sugar. So you've finally decided to shake a leg,' he drawled. 'I thought you'd be up at sunrise and ready to go.'

'I didn't sleep too well,' she excused herself. 'But don't dodge the issue, Dad. Did you or didn't you give Brad the sack last night?'

'No, I didn't. I promised you I wouldn't. When I went to see him he was packing up to leave. That was the arrangement he and I had, that he would leave us as soon as I arrived.' He raised the glasses to his eyes and looked at the freighter. 'Guess we're on a collision course with this guy and I'd best go to starboard of him. He has the right of way.'

He went to the instrument panel and turned a knob. Slowly the bow of the yacht swung to the right.

'Why wasn't I told of this arrangement you and Brad had?' demanded Carlotta shakily. 'Why didn't you tell me last evening?'

He didn't reply but raised the binoculars to his eyes again to watch the freighter going by on the port side of the yacht.

'Answer my question, please,' she insisted. 'And stop treating me as if I were a child. I'm all grown up now and can be told unpleasant truths. It's all right. I won't rush off in a huff and do anything you wouldn't like. I learned my lesson when I married Kurt against your advice. Please, Dad, why didn't you tell me you had that arrangement with Brad?'

He lowered the glasses again, turned the knob

on the instrument panel and the yacht's bow swung back on to the original course.

'I guess I thought he'd told you the other day after he'd talked to me and asked my permission to tell you why he'd been hired,' he replied smoothly. He gave her a sidelong glance. 'Were you mad when you found out he'd been hired as a bodyguard?'

'A little, but when he explained why I understood. I was really only mad at you for not telling me about those threats and taking me into your confidence, consulting me before hiring anyone to protect me.'

'I was anxious about you, honey. I had to do something quickly. I asked Skip to get in touch with Brad, to find out if he was still in Nassau and to ask him if he knew of anyone in the Caribbean area who could do the job of protecting you. Seems that Skip just caught Brad as he was getting ready to leave Nassau and fly to England. He'd finished working for the Bahamian police and was going home for Christmas. He didn't know of anyone suitable he could recommend to be your bodyguard but offered to come to Morunda, work on the yacht and keep an eye on you until I was able to get away or found someone who could take on the job of being your bodyguard permanently. I jumped at his offer. I'm sorry if you were miffed at not being consulted, but sometimes it's necessary to take action without consulting everyone involved. I did it for your safety. Does that answer your question?'

'I guess so,' she sighed. 'Have you found someone to be my permanent bodyguard?'

'No. And I'm not looking any more. The guy

who wrote the threatening letters has been found. He's some crazy nut who's got a grudge against the company because he was fired for not doing his work properly. He decided to take his revenge through me and you, although neither or us had anything to do with the hiring and firing of him. I guess you don't need a bodyguard . . .' he broke off then added drily, 'until the next time.'

'I'm glad I don't need a bodyguard any more and I hope there won't be a next time,' she said with vehement sincerity. 'But I'm sorry Brad had to leave so suddenly. He . . . he said he would try to let me know if . . . if there was to be a change, if he thought up some way of getting out of the embarrassment of us having to tell Phillida we had deceived her.'

'He said I was to say goodbye to you,' Mason replied, studying a sailing yacht they were passing. There wasn't much wind and the black-hulled, tan-sailed ketch was rolling idly on the sun-shimmered water. The helmsman raised his hand to wave to them. They waved back. 'I invited Brad to stay on as a guest to come to the Virgins and Puerto Rico, but he declined. He said he had to get back to England immediately.' Mason fiddled with the binoculars, adjusting the focus of the lens. He added casually, 'He's a nice guy, a helluva nice guy.'

'Yes, he is,' Carlotta mumbled and stared unseeingly out of the wide, grey-tinted glass at the distant horizon. She had thought she had plumbed the depths of despair last evening. But this feeling was worse. This was like being alive and dead at the same time.

A movement on the foredeck below the

wheelhouse drew her attention. Willy was sauntering along the deck towards the bow. He stopped to lean on the bulwark and looked over at the sparkling bow-wave. But no tall man with sun-bleached, dark brown hair followed him to lean beside him. Brad had left, was even now almost home, almost back in England, perhaps. He was miles away. A whole ocean separated him from her. Carlotta drew a long, shaky breath and let it out.

'What's wrong, honey?' Mason as always was quick to notice any emotional disturbance in his one and only child.

'Nothing much. I just wish . . .' She broke off and sighed again.'

'Go on. What do you wish?'

'That I wasn't a rich girl. That I was just an ordinary woman, with a career or some sort of work to do. I wish I had more freedom.' She turned to him. 'I'm glad I don't have to have a bodyguard any more. I'm glad you're here, too. It's such a long time since we were together. There's so much I want to talk to you about.'

'And I'm glad too, that you feel you want to talk to me,' he said, rather humbly for Mason J. Burr II, she thought. 'I guess I was a bit rough with you that day in Vienna.'

'Rough but right,' she admitted. 'I know now you were doing your best to prevent me from making a mistake. But you know, Dad, Granny Liz has always said about you that you only ever learned from making your own mistakes. Guess I must be like you.'

'Could be you are,' he agreed. 'Could be too, as my mother has pointed out to me more than once, I'm too possessive of you, over-protective too. But you see, Carlo, you're all I have left of my love affair and marriage with your mother. And then with being my heiress and all, it's only natural that I should want to try and stop you from falling into the traps set by creeps like Kurt Malden.'

'I understand that, and I guess I won't be any different when I'm a parent . . . if I ever am. But I can't help wishing I weren't your heiress. Life would be much simpler for me if I weren't. It would be easier to judge then if . . . if a man wanted to marry me because he really loved me. Do you understand what I'm getting at, Dad?'

'Only too well.' He laughed a little self-mockingly. 'Remember I was your grandfather's only son and heir. Come to think of it, I had this same discussion with him, when I was about twenty-one or two.'

'What did he do?'

'Sent me to work for the company as a rigger at an oil exploration site in the Arctic. Stopped paying me an allowance so that I had to learn to live on any income I earned. Made it known that I wouldn't be inheriting all he owned when he died.' He slanted her a glance. 'Is that what you want me to do? Cut your allowance, tell everyone you're not going to inherit billions of dollars?'

'You did threaten to do that when you found out I'd married Kurt,' she pointed out.

'It was a threat only and it was directed at him. And it worked, didn't it? Showed him up in his true colours?'

'Well, I've no wish to be an oil-rigger,' she said with a little laugh. Talking with him about her own situation like this was easing the cold leaden feeling, the feeling that something in her had died. 'I'm not that liberated. But I would like to see if I could do a job, earn an income and manage on it. I'm tired of being a little rich girl with nothing to do. The problem is I'm not much good at anything. I only know how to look after horses and ride them. I guess I'm pretty good at mucking out and riding.' She paused as a sudden idea flashed into her mind but decided not to tell him about it. Not yet. Not until she had written a letter and received an answer to it. Not until she was sure she had a job at a certain riding stables she knew of in England.

'Mucking out horses. Ha!' Mason's short laugh was derisive. 'Jobs don't come much dirtier than that. You could start your own riding school in Texas. I could finance you!'

'No. No. That's what I *don't* want! I have to go away, work somewhere on my own. You're not to come running with help, financial or otherwise. I'd like you to carry out your threat to stop my allownace—I haven't spent all you've given me, I've saved some and that will get me going. And I'd be very much obliged if you'd put it about that I'm not going to inherit all your millions. I don't want all of them anyway. There would be too much for just me.'

'My inheritance and yours, the ranch, the shares in the oil company aren't just for you, honey,' he argued softly. 'It's for your kids and their kids . . .'

'I won't be having any kids the way I'm going on,' she retorted suddenly losing patience. 'The way things are right now I'll never find the right guy to marry. Nice guys don't go hunting for rich girls.'

He swung to face her, grey eyes narrowing assessingly.

'You liked him a lot, didn't you?' he drawled. 'Too much.'

'What . . . what . . . who are you talking about?' she whispered blustering a little, realising at last that she had given herself away.

'You know what and who, honey,' he said drily. 'But you'll get over it. I wouldn't mind betting that by the end of next week you'll be over it. You always do get over these infatuations of yours in a few days.'

Her impulse was to flare up at him, to retort angrily, but just in time she remembered that was what she had done when he had warned her about Kurt. Now he had guessed how she felt about Brad and he was warning her again, not against Brad but against her own waywardness and changeability.

'Perhaps you're right,' she heard herself saying coolly. 'But that doesn't alter how I feel about being independent. Please, Dad, consider what I've said seriously. I don't want to have to go and find my way in the world without your blessing. I want us to stay friends. But I will go, I promise you that.'

'OK, I'm hearing you,' he replied with a touch of irritability. 'But you're not going yet. Wait until the end of this cruise we're going to take with Cora and Granny Liz. Talk over what it is you want to do with Granny. She has a lot of wisdom and her advice is worth taking.'

'Oh, I will, I will talk it over with her,' she said fervently. She was looking forward to seeing

her grandmother, who had stepped in and taken
the place of her mother when Juanita had died
so tragically. Granny Liz was bound to be on
her side in any arguments with Mason.

She glanced down at the foredeck again. Willy
was still there leaning on the rail and now she
imagined someone was beside him, as tall, wide-
shouldered man. Then the tall man turned.
Sunlight glinted on the streaks in his dark hair.
He looked up at the wheelhouse and it seemed
to her he looked right at her and gave her the
thumbs-up sign.

Her father spoke to her. The figure faded.
Only Willy was there. She turned with a smile to
answer Mason's question. She was feeling better.
An ocean might separate her physically from
Brad but something of him had remained with
her, in the depths of her heart.

CHAPTER TEN

On the first day of March, at the end of the cruise with her father, stepmother and grandmother, Carlotta left the yacht at Nassau and flew to England. She travelled light, taking with her the minimum of clothing. Her life as the spoiled heiress of Mason J. Burr was over. From that day on she would be an independent woman fending for herself and living on the small income she would earn as a riding instructor and stablehand at the stables in Berkshire owned by her grandmother's niece, Grace Heward.

Because she was just starting work at the stables, Grace let her live with her and her family in the old farmhouse where once Granny Liz had lived and grown up with her sister, Grace's mother, but by the end of May Carlotta had found separate accommodation and was sharing a small cottage in the nearby village with one of the other riding instructors, Sarah Goodall.

Although she had found going to work restrictive and routine at first, she had found many compensations working with the animals she loved and with companions with whom she had much in common. There had been pleasure too in watching spring work its magic on the English countryside, as drifts of daffodils had yellowed the grass in the orchard at Greenacres,

153

to be followed in May by the pale petals of fallen apple blossom. Lambs had been born to the few sheep Grace kept, and two new foals had been delivered in the stables. A robin had built its nest in the tangled garden of the cottage, and now swallows were flitting to and from the eaves.

Most of all Carlotta had enjoyed the privacy. No one at the stables or in the village knew she was the daughter of a billionaire oil tycoon. She was just a distant relative of Grace's from the States, a little different, it was true, with her drawling accent, her outspoken comments and her impulsive demonstrations of affection, but after the first few days she had been accepted and more or less ignored. Life was suddenly simple, there in the greenness of Berkshire. Her only social activity was a visit to the village pub on a Friday night with Grace and her husband Tom.

Slowly but surely the disasters of the previous months slipped from her mind. Kurt was forgotten. Bernard Digby was forgotten. Even Tizzy and Ethan had become vague. She was still hoping to forget Brad, but was reluctant to blot from her mind their crazy masquerade on New Year's Eve. Often when she was restless she would relive those moments when she had danced with him, and the way he had kissed her then and later on the shore at the Bay of Doves. Only when her memory began to remind her of the last time they had been together in his cabin did she open her eyes and try to think of something else. She didn't want to remember the remarks he had made when he had left her.

One afternoon in June, after the last of the

junior classes she had been instructing had finished, she sat in the tack-room, among the saddles and bridles, examining a bridle that had broken during the class. The door was pushed open and a man's voice said, 'I've come to pick up Joanna Martin. Do you know where she is?'

Carlotta gripped the bridle tightly, holding on to it as the only real thing to grasp. Was she going out of her mind? The voice sounded exactly like Brad's: cool, crisp. She looked up slowly at the doorway. She wasn't out of her mind. He was there, looking bigger somehow in a brown leather jacket, open-necked shirt and jeans. She stared at him feeling her heart begin to race and the blood to steal into her cheeks. He stared back.

'Carlotta?' he queried.

'Yes. It's me . . . I'm Carlotta,' she stammered and stood up. 'Joanna is in the stable, feeding sugar to her pony, I guess.'

His dark glance flashed over her in the way she remembered taking in her tightly bound hair, her sagging old sweatshirt and her stained jodhpurs and boots, before returning to her face. Kicking the door shut behind him, he stepped over to the table at which she was sitting.

'I didn't recognise you at first,' he said. 'You look a lot different from when I last saw you.' Again his glance frisked her. 'What are you doing here?' he asked.

'Isn't it obvious? I work here as a riding instructor.'

She sat down again because she felt suddenly weak. The room was vibrating with tension. She had a longing to fling her arms around him to hug him, she was so excited by seeing him again,

but the memory of one of his last remarks was
still branded on her mind. *Don't try it on with
me again*.

'It's unbelievable,' he murmured, and shook
his head from side to side so that the long lock
of hair slid over his forehead. The sun-bleached
strands weren't as noticeable and he wasn't
tanned any more. He looked as if he spent a lot
of his time working indoors.

'What is? That I'm working? Or that I'm
working here at these stables? I suppose you
always have thought I'm incapable of working
for my living and that I'm just a playgirl,' she
challenged him.

'I suppose I have,' he replied, his eyes glinting.
'You certainly never did anything when I was
with you to make me think otherwise!'

The longing to hug him and kiss him died a
violent death under the rush of an urge to slap
him for insulting her. She suppressed it with
difficulty and, turning away from him, picked up
the broken bridle.

'You'd best go and find Joanna,' she said
coldly. 'Good afternoon, Mr Bradley.'

He made no reply. She didn't look up but she
heard the latch of the door rattle as he lifted it.
Then the door slammed shut and he was gone.
Alone, she subsided shakily, folding her arms on
the table and putting her head down on them.
The unexpected meeting with Brad had shaken
her more than she would have believed possible.
The latch rattled and she straightened up quickly.
The door opened and Grace came in. Younger
looking than her forty-odd years, she was lean
and flat-chested. Her fair hair was scraped back
from her long thin face into a tight bun at the

back of her neck. She looked severe but her blue-grey eyes sparkled with humour.

'It's Colley's birthday today so I thought we'd take her out to dinner at the village pub tonight. Are you game?' she asked. Colley was one of the three riding instructors employed at the stables. 'Oh, dear, what's the matter?' The sparkle died in Grace's eyes as she glanced at Carlotta. 'You're as white as a ghost.'

'Perhaps that's because I've just seen one,' replied Carlotta, her voice unsteady. 'Did you see him, the man who just walked out of here? You must have passed him.'

'Yes, I did, as a matter of fact,' said Grace hitching a leg up on the corner of the table while she still studied Carlotta's white face. 'He nearly knocked me over. He seemed pretty angry about something. I've seen him before. Who is he? Did he come in here to see you?'

'He's Tristan Bradley and he didn't come to see me. He's come to pick up Joanna Martin. I suppose it's all right to let her go with him?'

'I expect he's come instead of her mother, Pat Martin. It's with her I've seen him occasionally, in Ascot. Gossip has it that they cohabit. You know what I mean? I've really no idea how to describe a relationship between a man and a woman when it's something like marriage but you know they aren't married, at least not to each other.' Grace paused and frowned a little. 'Now I come to think about it, Joanna could be his child. She does resemble him a little.' She looked across at Carlotta again. 'But that doesn't account for you thinking you saw a ghost when he came in here. Where and when did you meet him before?'

'In Morunda, when I was living on the yacht at the beginning of January.'

'Really? Well, what a coincidence him walking in and finding you here,' said Grace lightly.

'Yes, wasn't it,' murmured Carlotta, wondering whether it had been a coincidence. Was it possible Brad had known she was here at the stables? Who could have told him? Anyway, why would he go out of his way to come and see her? He had left her in no doubt, as usual, how he felt about her. She hurried after Grace and into the stableyard. A dark blue car was just driving away. From the passenger seat in front, dark-eyed and dark-haired, Joanna Martin waved to her and Grace. They both waved back.

'Grace, he knows about me,' Carlotta whispered as she walked with her cousin towards the farmhouse. Built of local reddish-brown brick, its old-fashioned sash windows outlined in white, it glowed in the sunlight of late afternoon among its attendant elm trees. 'He knows I'm Dad's heiress. I hope he doesn't tell Pat Martin who I am. I wouldn't want it to get around the village. I've been so happy living here, anonymous and ignored.'

'I wouldn't worry about her spreading gossip. She keeps very much to herself,' said Grace serenely. 'Now what time shall Tom and I pick you and Sarah up this evening?

Although Carlotta did her best to push the meeting with Brad to the back of her mind, it would keep forcing itself to the front. She tried hard to be merry at the dinner party and thought she was succeeding until she saw Brad walk into the pub's dining-room accompanied by a slim dark-haired, dark-eyed woman. Watching the couple covertly as they sat down at one of the dark oak tables, she nudged Grace.

'Is that Pat Martin?' she whispered. 'Look, over there. The table by the second window.'

Grace glanced around casually.

'Yes, that's her. And him. She's quite pretty, isn't she, but older than I had thought. Not much younger than I am, is my guess.' Grace turned back to the table and said sharply as Carlotta struggled to her feet, 'What are you doing? Where are you going?'

'I'm getting out of here,' muttered Carlotta. 'Sorry, Colley, Grace . . . I've just remembered something I have to do. See you tomorrow. See you later, Sarah.'

'Carlotta, you can't . . .' began Grace severely, but Carlotta paid no heed. The sight of Brad with another woman was proving too much for her just as the sight of him sitting with Tizzy had been one moonlit tropical night nearly six months ago. Jealousy was raging through her. She couldn't sit passively and see him smile at Pat Martin across candlelight. It was more than she could bear.

Once she had left the pub she turned along the lane to the cottage she shared with Sarah, forgetting she was wearing high heels, the first time for months. Finding she couldn't walk fast enough she took the shoes off and walked in her stockinged feet even though every tiny loose stone pricked her soles. As she walked she looked up at the starlit sky, at the moon, only in its first quarter and smaller than it was in the tropics. It was a lovely night, quiet, peaceful, an English midsummer's night when the fairies were supposed to come out and play havoc with the love lives of poor humans.

Well, they were certainly out tonight, Carlotta thought wryly as she let herself into the cottage. They had waved their wands and Brad had appeared, and now all the peace of mind she had worked so hard these past few months to achieve was gone. He had stepped into the tack-room that afternoon and the attraction she felt for him had been triggered off again. Of all the coincidences she could have imagined it was the last one she had expected when she had come to live in England. The chances of him coming to the place where she worked not knowing she was there were tens of thousands to one. No, more like a million to one. But if he had known, had found out in some way that she was working at Greenacres, why had he come to the stables? Just to check up on the information he had received that a young woman called Carlotta Burr was working there? Was it possible Joanna Martin—who could be his daughter, according to Grace—had mentioned her riding instructor's name to him?

That was it. That had to be it. He had heard her name at the home of his . . . his paramour, his mistress—God, what should she call Pat Martin? In the silence of her bedroom Carlotta ground her teeth. He had heard her name and had come to check her out and now he was probably telling Pat Martin all about her, laughing about her . . .

But he wouldn't tell Pat about their brief and tumultuous mating in his cabin aboard the *Montezuma*, would he? Oh, no. He wouldn't tell her of his physical conquest of the young woman whose bodyguard he had been for a few short weeks. Men were usually very secretive about such things. And often forgot them. As she must forget, as she was going to forget.

She slept badly and was tired and absent-minded the next day, going through the motions only of instructing children in how to ride. She left the stables late, long after Sarah had gone and walked back to the cottage slowly, in spite of the rain that had begun to fall.

She was quite a way from the cottage when a car coming the opposite way stopped beside her. The window rolled down and Brad looked out at her as he leaned over from the driver's seat. He pushed the door open.

'Get in,' he ordered.

'No, thanks. I've only a short way to go.'

'You'll get soaked.'

'I don't care.' She began to walk on. Behind her she heard the car door slam and expected to hear it move off, but instead she heard footsteps coming after her. Defensively she turned to face him.

'Carlotta, don't be silly,' he began, but his voice was soft and the little reddish flecks in his eyes had begun to glow. Grace was right, Joanna did resemble him a little, especially around the eyes. The implication of that resemblance hit her a hard and unexpected blow.

'But I am silly. And you know that . . .'

'You're bloody stubborn,' he growled at her. 'Come and get in the car. I'd like to talk to you. I was just driving out to the stables to see if you were still there.'

'There's nothing to talk about. We have

nothing to say to each other, Mr Tristan Bradley,' she said haughtily.

'Who told you my first name?' he demanded, looking disconcerted for a moment.

'My father. Goodbye.' She turned on her heel and began to walk on, pretending that one of her riding boots wasn't pinching her little toe.

Suddenly she was seized from behind. His hands at her waist he lifted her and threw her over his shoulder in a fireman's lift.

'Stop it, you bully,' she gasped hitting his back with both fists. 'Put me down.'

A car coming along the lane drew to a stop beside them. A man's voice asked if they needed help.

'No, thanks,' said Brad easily, turning to the man so that Carlotta was swung dizzily in the opposite direction. 'My wife has twisted her ankle and I'm just carrying her to the car.'

'OK.'

The car's window was closed, and the vehicle moved away slowly.

'Help, help,' yelled Carlotta breathlessly and almost at once she was lowered to her feet. They were right beside Brad's car.

'Shut up,' he snarled viciously, still holding on to her.

'Help, help,' she screeched. 'I'm being kidnapped.'

A sharp jerk and she was against him, breast to breast. Hard and domineering his lips came down on hers, smothering her next shout before it started.

The shock of his kiss, the unexpectedness of it also defeated any resistance in her before

she could make it. Her lips parted involuntarily
as she sighed with a feeling compounded of
delight and sudden amusement at this latest
escapade of theirs. She leaned against him
frankly, raised her hands to his nape and gave
in to the sensuous pleasure of being kissed by
him. After a while, when they both were
becoming aware that the rain was soaking their
hair, and drenching their clothing, Brad lifted
his mouth from hers. His dark eyes blazed
with fire.

'I had no intention of kissing you when I
stopped to give you a lift,' he murmured.

'And I had no intention of being kissed by
you,' she whispered. 'We couldn't help it.'

'It happened because you don't know how to
behave in an English country lane on a Sunday
afternoon,' he said roughly. 'Yelling for help
like that.'

'Well, what about you? Heaving me over
your shoulder as if I was . . . a sack of
potatoes,' she seethed. 'Kidnapping me.'

He laughed softly and, raising a hand, wiped
the rain from one of her cheeks with a
forefinger. At that remembered heart-touching
caress her knees shook. She wanted to shout at
him not to do it again, but all she could do was
stare at him as if mesmerised by the expression
of tenderness that had softened the hard lines
of his face.

'I've missed you, Carlotta, and I've been
anxious about you,' he murmured.

'Anxious about me? Why?' she exclaimed.

Immediately his face pokered up. It was as
if, for a moment, he had allowed her a glimpse
of someone she didn't know and had never

met and then had swiftly drawn down the
blinds. His face took on its usual expression,
eyes narrow and wary, line of mouth tightly
controlled.

'I can't tell you here, while we're getting
rained on. Isn't there somewhere we could go
to talk for a while? Somewhere out of the
rain?' he asked.

'You can come to the cottage. I share it with
Sarah. It's very small, though. And you'll have
to duck your head as you go through the
doorway.'

'It couldn't be any smaller than my cabin on
the *Montezuma*,' he said drily and, turning
away, he opened the nearest door of the car.
'Will you condescend now to get in?' he
drawled mockingly.

The drive to the cottage took no more than
four minutes. After parking the car on the
grass verge of the road, Brad followed her
along the flagged pathway between the tangled
flower beds to the plain front door under the
little peaked roof of the porch. He stood close
beside her as she unlocked the door. Inside
she lingered long enough in the narrow, dark-
panelled hallway to open the door to Sarah's
room to check whether or not her friend was
in. The room was empty so she closed the door
and went over to the door opposite.

As she entered her own room she whispered
to Brad, 'Don't forget to duck.'

Since it was such a damp evening she switched
on the electric fire and the simulated flames
began to flicker. A table lamp with a pink
shade dispersed gathering shadows and folk-
weave curtains pulled across the window blotted

out the greyness outside. Low-ceilinged, with heavy beams, the room was furnished with a wide settee, an armchair and a small, round dining table set under the window. In an alcove behind a curtain on one side of the fireplace were a sink and an electric cooker. On the other side of the fireplace was the door to the bedroom.

'Shall I shut the door?' Brad asked.

'Yes. And take off your jacket. The shoulders are wet. Hang it over one of those chairs,' Carlotta, determined to be practical, gestured towards the two Windsor chairs at the table. 'I'll get you a towel to dry your hair.'

Fifteen minutes later, her own hair drying and beginning to glint with golden sparks she sat curled up in the armchair. Brad sat down on the settee, leaned back, thrust his hands in his pockets and stretched his long legs before him, crossing his ankles. He looked up at the beams.

'This place must be quite old.' he said non-committally.

'About three hundred years, Grace says.'

'Grace?' His glance came down from the ceiling and focused on her.

'You know, she owns and runs the stables,' she replied coolly and went straight to the point. 'Brad, I have to ask you. Was it just coincidence we met this afternoon. Or did you know I was working at the stables?'

'I knew you . . . or I had heard that a Carlotta Burr was working there,' he said smoothly—too smoothly, she thought.

'So you came yesterday afternoon to check me out.'

'Right.'

'I suppose your . . . I mean, Joanna, mentioned my name.'

'She may have done.' He shrugged.

'She resembles you a little,' she murmured, rubbing at a spot on the knee of her jodhpurs, avoiding his gaze and feeling again the jealousy she had experienced the previous night in the pub's dining-room warping her thoughts. 'Is she your daughter?' As she spoke she flung back her head to look directly at him again.

'My what? Good God, no!' He sat up straight and stared at her. 'Where in hell did you get that idea?'

'Oh, it doesn't matter who suggested it to me, does it? You're very chummy with Joanna's mother, so it was a reasonable conclusion to draw from the child's resemblance to you,' she replied coolly, looking down at the spot on her knee again but watching him closely through the silky screen of her lashes.

'I see. Oh, I see very well,' he drawled, mockery glinting in his eyes. 'You've been listening to gossip. Pat told me there was talk about my regular visits to see her at the weekends and we had a good laugh about it.' He leaned back again but the mockery still danced in his eyes. 'So now I understand why you swept out of the pub last night, soon after we arrived.'

'I hadn't realised you'd seen me—you were so busy smiling at her, helping her to choose from the menu,' she said stiffly. 'I left because I didn't feel too well.'

'You'll always fail a lie detector test,' he jeered. 'You left the pub because you didn't like me paying more attention to Pat than to you. I haven't forgotten how you behaved the night we visited the Carters at Stenson Point. You haven't changed, Carlotta. You still show everything you feel, do everything up front, as they say in your country.' He gave her one of his dark, intent glances. 'And I'm glad,' he added softly.

'Is . . . is Pat Martin your mistress?' she asked.

He uttered his usual crisp oath and gave her a different glance, one that scorched her with scorn.

'Pat is my elder sister,' he replied.

'Oh.' She felt silly and relieved at the same time. 'You visit her a lot.'

'Because she's on her own a lot. Her husband is a master mariner, captains an oil tanker and is away months at a time,' he explained.

'Oh,' she said again, and felt herself colouring as she met the mockery glinting in his eyes.

'Feel better now?' he taunted.

'A little,' she admitted. 'Why . . . why didn't you tell me you would be leaving the *Montezuma* as soon as my father arrived?' she continued, returning to the attack.

'I'm not sure.' He spoke slowly, avoiding her eyes. 'Maybe I felt it was wiser not to.' He shrugged.

'And you broke your promise to let me know as soon as you thought up a way of avoiding telling Phillida about our masquerade, too,' she complained.

'There wasn't time to tell you or to say goodbye to you,' he said stiffly.

'I thought you left in a hurry because you

were glad to get out of an involvement with me,' she persisted. 'I guessed you'd regretted what had happened in your cabin from what you said to me about not trying it on again with you. You blamed me for what happened. You couldn't leave fast enough.'

'I left because I had to,' he interrupted her roughly. 'When we returned to Morunda there was a cable waiting for me at the marina. It was from my sister with the news that my father had died suddenly and asking me to fly home at once. That was why I left without saying goodbye to you. Mason made his plane and pilot available to me to fly me to Antigua that evening so I could catch a flight to Britain the next day.'

'Oh.' She felt even more deflated. 'He didn't tell me,' was all she could say. 'I'm sorry. About your father dying, I mean.'

There was a short, tense silence during which neither looked at the other. Then Brad said quietly, 'About what I said to you before I left you in my cabin, I was still trying to warn you, a little belatedly and after the fact, it's true, but I wasn't blaming you for what happened.'

'And that riddle about oil and water not mixing, what did you mean?' she asked hopefully. At least he was communicating with her, trying to explain.

'I was trying to tell you that there was no future for us as lovers or as a couple. I'd tried hard to keep you at a distance by being unpleasant to you, by insulting you and by flirting with Tizzy. I thought you'd get the message when I didn't knock on your cabin door that night you asked me to. It took a hell of a lot of will-power on my part not to walk right in and take what you offered.' His voice rasped drearily. 'And then in Basseterre I was sure you'd turned off.' He gave a gruff laugh. 'But I didn't reckon on *you* coming to *my* cabin.'

He sat up again and rested both elbows on his knees. His hands, forming a peaked roof above his eyes, screened their expression.

'What happened that afternoon was something that has never happened to me before,' he murmured. 'Whenever I've indulged in any sexual activity with a woman I've liked I've always been in control. I've always been cool enough to lay down the guidelines and to direct the affair my way. All I can say now by way of an apology to you is that I shouldn't have let it happen. Since I left Morunda I've gone through hell worrying about you.'

'Why?'

'Can't you guess?' he dropped his hands. The burning intent expression in his eyes made her pulses leap.

For a few moments she wasn't in the cottage room but in the small fo'c'sle cabin on the *Montezuma* with the sound of rushing water all about her. The flare-up of passion between them had been sudden and beautiful, the wildest of wild impulses she had ever experienced in the whole of her impulsive life, and apparently it had been the same for him. What had happened had been perfect in every way, a meeting of minds as well as bodies, a complete fusion of their two entities, a mating . . . Her thoughts screeched to a stop. Wide-eyed she stared at him.

'You . . . you were worried in case you had made me pregnant?' she gasped.

'I was,' he agreed very seriously. 'There wasn't time for me to take precautions and I couldn't be sure of you . . .' He broke off as she shook her head negatively from side to side.

In a silence broken only by the patter of rain against the window they gazed at each other, their eyes dazed as if both of them had been caught and trapped by the memory of what had happened one steamy tropical afternoon in a small cabin; as if they were both wishing it was happening again.

CHAPTER ELEVEN

BRAD was the first to move and to break the silence. On his feet in one brisk movement, he paced away into the darkest corner of the room.

'So are you?' he demanded harshly, swinging round to look at her from the shadows.

'No, I'm not,' she replied. 'I wish I were but I'm not.'

'Thank God for small mercies,' he said on a surging breath of relief and paced back to her. 'But what do you mean by saying you wish you were?'

Clear-eyed, she looked up at him. A smile twitched at the corner of her lips.

'I wish I were, because if I were you'd have to marry me' she said tauntingly. 'That's why you were worried, isn't it? You've been afraid I might turn up at your door and insist that you marry me because I would be having your child.'

'No, damn you. That isn't why I was worried. I was concerned in case you did something desperate to get rid of it, but mostly I was afraid you would never tell me about it. You see, I know about that queer pride of yours and I also knew I hadn't given you any reason to believe I cared about what you did after I'd left Morunda. I was so bloody anxious I wrote to you.'

'You wrote me a letter?' she whispered. 'When?'

'Must have been beginning of March some time, when I guessed you would be back in Texas,' he replied, hands in his pockets as he paced around the room again.

'I came here on March 1st,' she said rather mournfully.

'I know. Your father told me that when he sent my letter to you back to me. He told me you were living and working at Greenacres Stables and asked me to look you up.' He paused in front of her again, slanted a derisive glance in her direction. Now that he had ascertained that she wasn't pregnant he seemed to have recovered his usual arrogance. 'He suggested I kept an eye on you, saw you didn't get into any mischief or take up with any undesirable characters,' he announced mockingly.

'Oh, hell.' The usual irritation with her father boiled through her. 'Why must he be so damned interfering? I came here to get away from his smothering all-protective attitude,' she raged. 'I came here to be independent, to prove to him and anyone else who cares to know that I'm not just a rich playgirl and that I don't want to be. So he had to write you and tell you where I am!' She broke off, her breast rising and falling as she still seethed with anger. He had walked away from her during her outburst and was picking up his jacket from the chairback over which he had hung it. He slipped it on.

'Where are you going?' she asked unsteadily.

'Back to London. I have to work tomorrow,' he said curtly. He zipped his jacket and strode towards the door. In a flash she was out of the chair and had slid between him and the closed door. Her back to the door, she faced him, her chin up her head high, her loosened hair shimmering like raw silk against the dark, oak panelling of the old door.

'I'll see you again?' she asked. Although she spoke in her usual, imperious rich-girl manner, inside she was miserably aware that she had offended him in some way and he had withdrawn from her, just when he had seemed on the verge of admitting he was in love with her.

'Not if you don't want to. Since you've just made it very clear how you regard my keeping an eye on you as your father suggested in his letter, why should I hang around here?' he retorted. 'He isn't paying me to be your bodyguard any more, you know.'

'Mercenary,' she hissed.

'A guy makes his living the best way he can. We aren't all born heirs or heiresses to a fortune,' he jibed. 'Now, just stand aside, Carlotta, and I'll be on my way.'

'Before you go you have to give me my letter,' she insisted.

'What letter?' His face was impassive, the face of an officer from an élite security force, trained to be tough and watchful.

'The letter you wrote to me, of course.' She held out one hand to him, palm upwards. 'Give it to me.' If she could get it and read it she might get some clue as to his real feelings about her, she thought.

'I tore it up and threw it away,' he replied blandly, looking her right in the eyes, his own eyes absolutely without expression, dark, soulless.

'Oh, I guess you pass all the lie-detector tests

with flying colours. Get high grades all the time
for lying without a flicker of an eyelid,' she
sniped. Then, hands to her cheeks, she said
more shakily, 'Oh, that was a mean thing to do
out of the many mean things you've done and
said, to write me a letter and then not let me
have it, to tear it up and throw it away. It goes
with you being glad that I'm not pregnant with
your child.'

'I didn't say I'm glad you're not.' The breath
he drew was sharp, giving her hope that her
taunt had found a target.

'Relieved, then.'

His face was rigid, bone showing white along
the angle of his jaw, lips a compressed line,
eyelids lowered, a blind implacable face. Carlotta
shivered. He seemed more like her enemy than
her lover.

'Is there someone else?' she asked in a quieter,
humbler way. 'If there is, if you have a woman
already, hidden away somewhere in London,
whom you love and to whom you're committed,
I'll understand and I'll bow out of the picture as
gracefully as I can.'

'There is no one else,' he replied slowly.
'There was once, but the affair ended when I
asked her to marry me.'

'When you asked her . . .?' she exclaimed and
broke off as surprise choked her voice. Wide-
eyed she gazed up at him. Some of the hardness
had gone from his face. One corner of his lips
lifted in a familiar self-mocking smile. 'Why?'
she croaked. 'Why did she turn you down?'

'She didn't like the job I was doing. I was in
the security force then. She didn't like the
violence involved, the guns I might have to use,

the shift work.' He shrugged. 'There was a lot she didn't like about the job, but I think that really she had found out she didn't like me. She just used the job as an excuse to get out of the arrangement we had. She married someone else a month after we split.' The cynicism in his expression increased. 'Someone she could push around. Since then I haven't let myself become too serious about any woman. Short, casual affairs have been the order of the day.' He cocked a sardonic eyebrow. 'Got that?'

'Yes, I have. Very clearly. Another insult to add to the long list of insults you've handed out to me one way or another ever since I asked you to dance with me on New Year's Eve,' she raged.

His face took on its shuttered expression again. 'There's nothing to be gained by that sort of recrimination,' he retorted coldly. 'I'm sorry if you've felt insulted by anything I've said. Or done. I've tried to explain what I was doing, keeping you at a distance because there could be no future for us together.'

'The oil and water bit again?' she challenged jeeringly, and watched him closely. There was turbulence behind the impassivity. It was showing in the flare of red light in his eyes, in the twitch of a muscle at the corner of his mouth.

'Someone once put it better than I did,' he murmured. 'Someone once said rich girls don't marry poor boys.'

'And that's a lot of sentimental garbage,' she retorted, pushing away from the door and standing so close to him the tips of her breasts brushed against his jacket. Her eyes on the pulse beating madly at the base of his throat, she played with the zip of his jacket. 'Anyway, I'm not rich. I'm just a riding instructor at Greenacres Stables earning a few quid a week, and I'm still in love with you.' She glanced up at him through her lashes, half-smiling.

He didn't bend his stiff neck nor did he smile back at her but he closed his eyes so he couldn't see her.

'You're still Mason J. Burr's daughter and I thought I told you never to try it on again with me,' he said in his brisk Scotland Yard voice.

'But Dad isn't paying you any more. You don't owe him anything. No service, no loyalty,' she argued; and slid both hands around his neck to the nape. Her fingers enjoyed playing with his thick hair. 'As for me not trying it on again with you, what else can I do? It's the only weapon I have against your pride,' she whispered. 'I love you, Brad, I've had a few months away from you to find that out. I haven't changed my mind about you. I realised that when you walked into the tack-room yesterday. And I think you love me, just a tiny little bit, don't you?''

He answered her by kissing her as she had hoped he would, but as his hard lips claimed the softness of hers possessively and she leaned invitingly against him, they both heard the cottage door open, the high voice of Sarah followed by the deeper voice of Sarah's boyfriend Kenny.

Immediately Brad withdrew, raised his head and pushed her away. Alert and tense he slanted her an enquiring glance.

'It's only Sarah and Kenny. They won't come in here. Sarah has her own room,' she explained. 'Brad, don't go. Stay and have supper with me.

Stay the night. You can easily get to London from here in the morning.'

'You don't know what you're asking——' he started to argue roughly.

'Yes, I do. I'm asking you to stay and sleep with me. Oh, why do you persist in making it so hard for me?'

'Because you're right. I do love you,' he almost snarled at her, passion breaking through his control at last. 'Too much to have a casual affair with you. Too much to meet in secret. Too much to pretend . . .'

'Then why not ask me to marry you?' she interrupted him stormily.

He didn't bother to hide his scorn of her suggestion. It showed in the curl of his lower lip, in the way his glance raked her.

'I doubt if you could get by on my salary,' he jibed.

'Try me?' she challenged.

'No.'

They were facing each other like enemies again and she couldn't bear it. She flung herself at him, wrapping her arms around him, hiding her face against the tough leather of his jacket so that he wouldn't see the tears that had sprung to her eyes.

'How mean can you get?' she whispered unsteadily. 'How . . . how can I have your babies if . . . if you won't marry me?'

His chest rose and fell as he sighed. She felt his fingers in her hair, stroking it, then they were under her chin, forcing her face up so he could see it. She looked up, her own eyes starred with tears looking into his, which held a tortured expression. With a forefinger he stroked away one tear that had spilled on to her cheek.

'Blackmail?' he queried, with a lift of one eyebrow.

'Yes. I . . . I'm very old-fashioned and I'm not sleeping with you if I can't have a baby. I'm not taking precautions and I never have.'

'Then I'd better leave right now.' Hands at her waist he pushed her away again.

'*Brad!*' She almost screeched his name in her agony. She caught hold of his arms and gripped them hard. 'Oh, you'll be sorry if you go now,' she went on in a low shaky voice. 'You'll be really sorry if you leave me now and when they tell you the next time you come to pick up Joanna that I'm not here, that . . . that I've done the Ophelia thing and drowned myself.'

Her voice faltered and tears brimmed again as she saw his jaw was rigid. Letting go of him, she turned away and trailed over to the settee. She sank down on it and smoothed a hand over the place where he had so recently sat, seeking comfort from the warmth he had left there. 'It's because I'm an heiress to Dad's loot, isn't it?' she moaned. 'You don't want anyone to think you're a fortune-hunter like Kurt.'

'That's part of it,' he admitted.

'And the other part?'

He swung round to face her, regarding her from under frowning brows.

'My job. I'm not in the unit any more. I don't have to go out with a gun to protect a place or person where there's been a threat of a terrorist attack. I'm in a more consultative, administrative position, but I'm still involved with security. I still deal in violence or, at least, the attempt to prevent violence. And I like my job. I'm not prepared to give it up.'

'I see.' Bitterness seared her. 'So I've to suffer because my father is wealthy and some stupid little girl, way back in your past, refused to marry you because you were a security cop. Thanks. Thanks a lot for that.' Her voice shook, the tears spilled and she swayed against the back of the settee, hands covering her face as she was riven by a storm of emotion such as she had never known before. 'Oh, God, what am I going to do?' she muttered. 'I might as well be dead if . . . if I can't live with you, be a part of your life, no matter how unimportant.'

She didn't hear him stride across the room. The first she knew that he was near to her was the sinking of the settee cushions beneath his weight when he sat beside her. Hands gentle on her shoulders he lifted her away from the back of the settee and held her to face him.

'You're not the only one who would suffer,' he said unsteadily. 'Do you believe I wouldn't suffer too, that I haven't already suffered . . .?'

'But why should we suffer?' she argued, flinging back her head to look into his eyes. 'Why shouldn't we have each other, love each other while we can?'

Her eyes brimmed again and he groaned. Cupping her chin with one hand he kissed her hard on the mouth, his lips pressing hers until her own lips surrendered and parted to the scorching heat of the kiss. Slowly his lips left hers to kiss each tear away from her smooth, golden cheeks with a tenderness she would never forget. From her cheeks to her eyes his lips wandered where he licked away the tears that had not yet fallen, then from one temple to the other before sliding down one cheek again to the corner of her lips. With a long, sobbing sigh she turned her head and their lips met again, salt with her tears.

Against the back of the settee they leaned, still kissing. From her waist to her breast his hand moved, enclosing it with long tensile fingers. At that tenderly marauding touch all her frustrated love for him gushed forth. Her hands became busy too, slipping undone shirt buttons, sliding inside the shirt's opening, her fingers curling against the mat of dark hairs, nails digging into flesh that seemed to be on fire with his desire.

Long ago in the cabin on the *Montezuma* they hadn't spoken because no words had been needed. No words were needed now. Anyway, when they spoke to each other they said all the wrong things, thought Carlotta dreamily, as he lifted her in his arms and carried her through to the dark bedroom.

Lying on the bed, they communicated through hot, blistering kisses and subtly seeking caresses. His warm fingers sliding over her bare skin sent erotic sensations tingling through her and desire began to swell slowly and pleasurably within her.

It was different from the swift, rocketing union they had experienced on the yacht. There was no panic, no lack of time, no fear that someone might knock on the door. Every subtle caress became a fulfilment in itself, was a pleasure to be savoured, but inevitably the demand for closer communication grew in both of them, rising throbbingly until both of them were aware no longer of where they were—in a yacht's cabin with the sea rushing by or in a cottage bedroom on the creaking bed with the rain pattering at the window.

For a while, after it was done, they lay still and silent, she curled up with her back to him in the shelter of his arms. Only when she felt his fingers playing with her hair did she speak.

Softly, yet tauntingly she said, 'Now, you'll have to marry me.'

His answer was to kiss her shoulder, then the side of her neck, then her ear. She turned to face him, wishing she could see him.

'What does it matter who thinks you're a fortune-hunter as long as I know you're not,' she whispered. 'As long as I know you're not going to desert me when you find out that Dad has stopped my allowance and is changing his will so that his fortune will be spread out and I won't get everything. Anyway, he isn't going to die for years and years yet. Given his health and vitality he'll probably live until he's over ninety and it'll be our children who'll inherit everything. As for your job, I don't mind about that. I know you're doing something that is necessary these days. I'll hate it only when it takes you away from me, but I intend to go on working here, at the stables, for as long as I can, and I'm willing to put up with being separated from you for short periods of time because separation will make getting together so much more exciting. I promise you, you'll never get bored being my *real* husband!'

His mouth claiming hers again in hard possession stifled the rest of her running commentary, and happily she submitted again to the mastery of his love-making until, through the tumultuous sound of her heart in her ears, she thought she heard a voice calling to her. Sarah's high soprano. It was near. In the next room!

Sitting up sharply Carlotta gasped, 'Sarah!' and then bounded from the bed. She snatched her dressing-gown from the curtain-covered clothes alcove, wrapped it around herself and darted into the living-room, closing the door on the sound of Brad's muffled laughter.

Sarah, pink-cheeked from hovering over a cooker, was standing in the middle of the living-room staring at Brad's jacket, which he had tossed carelessly over the arm of the settee.

'What do you want?' Carlotta demanded.

'I . . . oh.' Startled, Sarah looked away from the jacket and at Carlotta. Her wide, china-blue eyes widened even more as she noted Carlotta's tangled hair, poppy-red bruised lips, hastily donned dressing-gown and bare feet. 'Kenny and I are having spaghetti and meat sauce for supper and I don't have any basil or Parmesan cheese. Could I borrow them from you?' As if drawn by a magnet, Sarah's eyes swerved back to the incriminating man's jacket.

'Yes, I have.' Carlotta went quickly to the cooking alcove opened a wall cupboard, searched for and found both basil and Parmesan. She thrust them at Sarah who was still mesmerised by the jacket. 'There you are. Now, go. I can smell your sauce burning.'

'Oh, gosh.' Whirling, Sarah ran for the door, but looked back before she closed it and added impishly, 'You look awfully pretty, Carlo, when you've been kissed.'

The door slammed shut and the cushion that

Carlotta had grabbed and flung at Sarah fell to the floor, never having reached its target. For a second Carlotta stood glaring at the door, fuming inwardly, then slowly she began to grin, remembering her own hasty rush from the bedroom. As if it mattered that Sarah had guessed she had been with a lover in the bedroom! Neither Sarah nor Kenny made a secret of their relationship. They did everything up front.

'So what do you have in mind for *my* supper tonight? drawled Brad from the bedroom doorway and she turned to look at him. He was buttoning his shirt.

'You're going to stay then?' she said hopefully, going over to him.

'Only for supper . . . and then I must go.'

'But you'll . . . you'll come again, next weekend . . . or even during the week.' She put her arms around him and rested her head against his chest. 'I . . . I'll be a very good wife. I've been well trained by my grandmother. I'll always be here when you need me. I like cooking and I'm pretty good at it . . .'

'So how about proving that now,' he murmured. 'I'm ravenous!'

'OK!'

He went back into the bedroom and she went to search cupboards for food, singing softly to herself. She had won. She had overcome his stubborn resistance. She heard him come back into the room and, checking that the food she was preparing was cooking, she went over to the table and began to set it.

'When we're married,' she began.

'I haven't asked you yet,' he said softly and she flinched giving him a wide wary glance.

'But . . . but . . .' She stammered and stopped. 'I'm sorry,' she went on more humbly. 'I tend to jump ahead and . . . and . . .'

'Make assumptions,' he supplied. 'That's because you're used to having your own way.' She must have looked crestfallen because he came over to her and smiled down at her. 'Don't worry, sweetheart. I'm going to ask you to marry me, but in my own way and when I'm ready. It's going to take me a while to adjust to the idea and then there is the matter of having to write to Mason J. Burr.'

'This has nothing to do with him. Nothing at all,' she said tautly.

'Will you let me finish?' he admonished her gently, yet sternly. 'The way I propose marriage, it has a lot to do with him. You claim to be old-fashioned. Well, I claim to be a traditionalist and although I know it isn't considered to be necessary these days, I'm going to write to Mason to tell him we're going to be married and to ask for his blessing. It will show him courtesy and respect and will perhaps convince him I'm not a fortune-hunter.' He smiled at her again. 'Please bear with me, love. I am what I am and it's too late in the day for me to change my ways.'

He touched her cheek with one finger. She grabbed and held the finger then pressed his hand against her lips for a second.

'Dad said you're a nice guy and I agree with him,' she said. 'I'll bear with you. I'll put up with your rocklike pride, your cynicism, your reserve and your job as long as you'll hold me in your arms often, sometimes kiss me, keep me safe and say you love me.'

'I love you, capricious Carlotta,' he said, his voice unsteady. 'I've loved you from the day I first set eyes on you in Morunda,' he confessed. 'It's just been hard to believe that you love me in the same way. Even now . . . I can't be sure that you won't change your mind about me once we're married.'

Shaken by his confession, and dismayed by his lack of confidence in her, Carlotta did the only thing she could: she showed her affection by flinging her arms around him and kissing him, but because they kissed too long supper wasn't the success she had planned. The steaks were overdone and the sauce burned. By the time Brad got up from the table to go she was almost in tears again, convinced he wouldn't come back because he didn't like her cooking.

Following him to the door, she said urgently, 'I don't know where you live. I have no address or telephone number. I don't know how to get in touch with you if . . . if I need to.'

He turned back to her, slanted her a thoughtful glance and slowly put his hand in the slit pocket of his jacket and brought out a rather crumpled envelope. He handed it to her.

'My address and telephone number are in that.' As she took it from him he bent and kissed her temple. 'See you, soon, lover,' he whispered.

He went while she was still staring at the envelope. It was addressed to herself at the Burr ranch in Texas. It was the letter he had written to her. The devil had lied to her when he had said he had torn it up and thrown it away! Her heart jumping, she went over to the armchair, curled up in it, slit the envelope open and took out the single page of notepaper.

'My dear Carlotta,' she read, and could hear his voice in her ears, soft and deep as it had been when he had admitted to loving her. 'I had to leave the yacht and fly home without saying goodbye to you,' the letter continued, going straight to the point. 'That's bothering the hell out of me. I can't help thinking you must believe I'm a complete bastard for not having more control when you came to my cabin. The truth is, sweetheart, I have never felt for any woman what I felt for you at that moment in time. Your beauty, the heat, your closeness to me in that small cabin were too much for me. I gave in to the longing I had to love you and, well, you know what happened.

'No one knows more than I do that a great gulf separates us. You're a wealthy heiress accustomed to having everything you want, everything money can buy. You've been sheltered and protected all your life. You're lovely, naïve and innocent. My background has been very different and I am none of the things you are, but I guessed early on in our acquaintance that Kurt had been rough with you, and I felt compassion for you. I could have killed him, if he hadn't been dead already, for violating you.

'But to get back to the reason for this letter. Please write and let me know how you are. We both behaved recklessly that afternoon without thought for any consequences. The thought now that you are pregnant and possibly considering doing something to get rid of the pregnancy is making me sweat with horror. Please write and tell me the truth about yourself and don't do anything before I come to you. Sincerely, Brad.'

For a long time Carlotta sat with the letter in her hand. Now she knew she was truly loved by the man she loved. It was the driving force of passionate love that had made him write this letter, had made him drop the barrier of his cool reserve and admit that he cared about what happened to her and about what had happened during her day-long marriage to Kurt.

The letter convinced her that Brad would be back, but she had to wait three long weeks before she saw him again. During that time she received a phone call from Texas, from Mason telling her that he had received a letter from Brad asking his permission to propose marriage to her.

'So what are you going to do?' she asked cautiously.

'I've written back to say I'll be happy to attend your wedding to him whenever you decide to have the ceremony,' he replied, equally cautious.

'Oh, Dad, thank you, thank you, thank you!' Carlotta couldn't stay cautious for long.

Not having heard from Brad she was thinking she would have to go up to London to find him when he turned up one Saturday afternoon at the stables.

'I've come for Joanna,' he said. 'And also to ask you out to dinner. The time has come for me to propose.' He glanced around the stableyard where girls were heaving saddles off horses and shouting at each other. Looking back at her, he suddenly lost his casual pose. Little red sparks began to flare in his eyes as he stepped close to her. 'I was going to do it over candlelight and wine glasses, to soft music,' he murmured. 'But I can't wait any longer.' He grasped both of her hands in his. 'Will you marry me, Carlotta of the golden eyes and golden hair, and will you have my babies?'

The mockery that rippled through his voice and danced in his eyes didn't offend her because she knew now that it hid the burning sincerity of his love for her.

'Oh, Tristan,' she mocked back, 'I thought you'd never ask.' Then sobering, she looked up at him all the love she felt for him expressed in her eyes. 'I'll marry you with pleasure,' she whispered.

Heedless of the curious stares of the suddenly silent girls, he swept her against him and kissed her hard and she kissed him back, thankful that there was no need for pretence or secrecy, that the masquerade begun on a wild impulse months ago was going to become a reality at last.

Incurable romantics, read one before bedtime.

Josephine, Jane and Jacinth were a trio of friends who as students at the Princess Beatrice Hospital in London shared the first years of hard work, laughter and tears.

But now the training is over and the time has come for them to go their separate ways as fully fledged nurses and midwives.

Take Three Nurses is a series of three stories that follow the individual fortunes of each of the three girls on the road to success and romance.

Josephine and a Surgeon of Steel

Jane and the Clinical Doctor

Jacinth and The Doctor Make a Wish

Available from April '87 Price £3.30

ROMANCE

Next month's romances from Mills & Boon

Each month, you can choose from a world of variety in romance with Mills & Boon. These are the new titles to look out for next month.

THE SHADOW OF MOONLIGHT Lindsay Armstrong
DREAM OF LOVE Kay Clifford
SINGLE COMBAT Sandra Field
FANTASY UNLIMITED Claire Harrison
THE EAGLE AND THE SUN Dana James
A SAVAGE ADORATION Penny Jordan
CIRCLE OF FATE Charlotte Lamb
HAY FEVER Mary Lyons
TOUCH AND GO Elizabeth Oldfield
BROKEN SILENCE Kate Walker
*****A DANGEROUS PASSION** Jayne Bauling
*****NO STRINGS ATTACHED** Annabel Murray

Buy them from your usual paperback stockist, or write to: Mills & Boon Reader Service, P.O. Box 236, Thornton Rd, Croydon, Surrey CR9 3RU, England. Readers in Southern Africa — write to: Independent Book Services Pty, Postbag X3010, Randburg, 2125, S. Africa.

*These two titles are available *only* from Mills & Boon Reader Service.

Mills & Boon
the rose of romance

They were from different worlds...

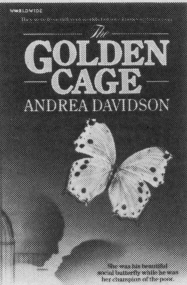

...and yet nothing could keep them apart.

Elizabeth Parkins lived among the elegant surroundings in Chicago's North Shore.

Sam Winslow lived among the unfortunate souls destined to live in the city's decaying slums.

They would risk everything they believed in, just for the one chance to be together ... **W◉RLDWIDE**